Born in Geraldton, Western Australia, Amanda moved to Perth, Western Australia, to study film & television and creative writing at Murdoch University, earning a BA in Communication Studies. Perth has been her home ever since, aside from a nineteen-month stint in London, England, where she dabbled in Film & TV 'Extra' work.

Amanda is a Scribe Award winner, a two-time Tin Duck Award winner, an Aurealis and Ditmar Award finalist, who primarily writes in the science fiction and thriller genres.

Her works include the sci-fi crime thriller, *The Subjugate*, which is being developed for TV by Anonymous Content and Aquarius Films. *The Subjugate* is also being studied at two German universities (Düsseldorf and Cologne) as part of a program on Australian speculative fiction, in conjunction with the Centre for Australian Studies.

Amanda wrote the Scribe Award winning procedural thriller, *Pandemic: Patient Zero*, which was the first novel set in the *Pandemic* board game universe.

She's also written for Marvel in their X-Men universe, as well as for Black Library in their Warhammer 40k universe.

To keep up to date with new releases visit:
amandabridgeman.com.au

I0601124

Also by Amanda Bridgeman

Aurora Series
#1 Aurora: Darwin
#2 Aurora: Pegasus
#3 Aurora: Meridian
#4 Aurora: Centralis
#5 Aurora: Eden
#6 Aurora: Decima
#7 Aurora: Aurizun
#8 Aurora: Atlas

Salvation Series
#1 The Subjugate
#2 The Sensation

Spud Compton Series
#1 The Darkest Cargo
#2 The Deepest Jungle
#3 The Deftest Deceit

The Time of the Stripes

Pandemic
Patient Zero

Marvel: School of X
Sound of Light

SHORT STORIES

Marvel: School of X anthology
Eye of the Storm

Inferno! Presents: The Emperor's Finest
Reconsecration

THE DEEPEST JUNGLE

SPUD COMPTON #2

AMANDA BRIDGEMAN

COPYRIGHT

The Deepest Jungle
EPUB format: 978-0-6482162-8-5
Print format: 978-0-6457363-1-1

Original cover design by
Amanda Pillar of Smoking Hot Covers

CHAPTER ONE

Spud Compton, freshly discharged from the med bay, walked down one of the long corridors of the admiral's ship, Gabriel, his shoulders heavy with the burden of what he had to do. Given all his belongings were on his impounded ship, Benobi-451, he'd been given a Galactic Force navy uniform from the Gabriel's supply. He felt uncomfortable wearing the uniform again. He'd left his old one behind several years ago with no plan to ever wear it again. Now here he was. He could just imagine how pleased his father would be to see him in it.

He found his way to the cabin on the lower decks where he'd been told he would find Finn. He knocked on the open door and looked inside to see his crewman lying in bed, shirtless, but bandaged. He looked a lot better than when Spud had last seen him—with his chest torn up by the Panthera-X03's claws.

"Hey," Spud said, "can I come in?"

"Sure," Finn said, sitting up and scratching fingers through his short, dark hair as Spud entered.

Spud walked over to grab the lone chair in the small, grey-walled cabin and sat down beside Finn's bed. "How you doing?"

"Better. They gave me some kind of anti-venom."

"Yeah, me too."

Finn nodded. "I heard you got clawed. Your back, right?"

"Yeah," Spud nodded, eyeing Finn's bandaged chest. "I suspect getting clawed on the back was a little easier than on the chest."

"Not gonna lie," Finn said, "it hurt like hell."

Spud grimaced, remembering the searing pain as the claw marks seem to burn his skin. "The venom's pretty toxic. It almost killed us."

Finn nodded, peeling back his bandages to show Spud his wounds. "It's healing pretty fast, though. Like, faster than they expected. It barely hurts now. Must be something in the anti-venom?"

"Yeah." Spud eyed Finn's almost-healed wounds, four gnarly thick pink lines that angled down from his upper chest to his belly. "But, hey, I'm told chicks dig scars, so..."

Finn smiled briefly before it faltered again. He looked back at Spud with serious eyes. "King and Miguel... They didn't make it."

"No." Spud's eyes dropped to the floor and he felt an imaginary clamp tighten around his chest, before looking back at Finn. "They both died saving my life."

Finn gave a sad smile. "You were always saving

King's. He told Nikita he owed you."

They heard a knock on the door and turned to see Nikita and Glossy, his remaining *Benobi* crew, enter.

"Is it true?" Nikita demanded, storming up to Spud, her brown eyes glaring fiercely at him.

"They can't send us down there, can they?" Glossy chimed in, equally intense.

Spud held his hands up to stop them. "Ladies—"

"What's going on?" Finn asked between them.

Nikita stared at him, crossing her dark muscular arms, while Glossy paced and ran her hand over her closely shaved, bright-pink hair.

"They're going to let us off the theft charges," Spud explained to Finn, "if we do a mission for them."

"Who?" Finn asked. "The navy?"

Spud nodded.

"Some mission!" Glossy exclaimed. "They're sending us down to a planet *filled* with X03s!"

"They what?!" Finn looked at Spud.

"Now, hold on," Spud said. "There're only... *five* of them."

"Five!" Finn's eyes popped. "What the hell? We barely survived one!"

Spud held his hand up again. "Look I'm not happy about this either, but we don't have much choice. It's rot in jail or do this and we're off the hook."

Finn pulled himself to sit up straighter. "Spud, what the hell are we supposed to do against *five* of those things? There are only four of us left."

"Five," Spud said. "Lieutenant Grey's coming with us. And... they're sending us in with Tiberius' unit."

"Tiberius!" Glossy exclaimed.

"Your brother?" Finn asked.

Spud nodded. "The navy is sending their hero soldier to protect us."

"If Tiberius is going in, why do they need us?" Glossy asked.

"I asked the same question," Spud told them. "We have experience with the Panthera-X03. Tiberius doesn't."

"How did your brother get involved with this?" Nikita asked.

"When Grey told the navy I was aboard the *Benobi* and used me as collateral for them not blowing us up, the navy contacted my father. Probably to save their asses. He negotiated the deal for our release with no charges."

"Your father would rather send you to face five Panthera-X03s than sit safely in jail?" Finn asked.

Spud nodded. "I guess he thinks my brother will save my ass. Or," he shrugged, "he's trying to suck me back in to the military."

"But you don't want that," Nikita said. Spud looked at her. Nik was his best friend; knew him better than anyone.

"No," Spud said, "I don't." He sighed. "I mean, I don't know the details of this. The X03 is a black ops secret, right? Would the navy even tell my father what this mission is?"

"We really don't have a choice in this?" Finn asked. "It's either jail or face the Pantheras?"

Spud nodded glumly.

Finn sighed and looked down at the four raised healing scars slashed down his skin.

"How's your back?" Nikita asked Spud. "Are you even in any state to do this?"

Spud shrugged his shoulders. "The skin feels a little tight, but I'm otherwise okay."

"Your wounds are healing really fast," Glossy said, intrigued.

Spud nodded. "They gave us their best and most expensive treatments to get us on our feet as soon as possible." Spud rubbed at the stubble on his jaw. "Now we know why."

Finn and Spud exchanged a look, as Finn scratched his hand through his hair again and sighed.

"So, when do we go?" Finn relented.

"As soon as my brother gets here."

"I cannot believe this," Nikita shook her head.

"We're all going to die," Glossy said.

"No, we're not," Spud said. "You guys are going to be the extraction team. You're going to drop us off and stay on the ship ready to pull us out."

"You're going in without us?" Nikita's eyes bored into his.

"I'm not getting more of my crew killed, Nik. I got us in this mess. It's my problem."

"Spud..." Glossy's eyes shone.

"Hey," Spud stood, "the great Tiberius will be there to protect me. I'll be fine." He squeezed Glossy's shoulder, then glanced back to Finn. "Get dressed. We'll rendezvous in an hour."

Spud walked aimlessly along the crew cabin corridors of the *Gabriel*. He wasn't sure where he was going, but he just needed to walk.

And try and figure a way out of this mess.

Memories of the Panthera-X03 aboard the *Benobi* flashed through his mind: he saw Grey's soldiers being torn apart; saw Miguel fall, trying to stab his kitchen knives into the beast; saw Finn's torn up chest, the blood. He saw King fall, the flamethrower having failed him; saw King die in his arms; recalled the pain he'd felt as the X's claws had slashed down his back.

"Spud!" he heard Grey's voice call.

He blinked, wondered if he was still caught up in memories.

"Spud!" Grey called his name again. He turned around and saw her approach. Dressed in her uniform, blond curly hair tied back in a bun, her green eyes were fixed on his.

She was a sight for Spud's sore eyes.

"Hey," she said softly, catching up to him, "there's a transmission for you. It's your father."

"My father?" Spud placed his hands on his hips. "Well, shit, I haven't heard from him in a while. What a nice surprise."

Grey gave a brief smile at his sarcasm. "There's a comms room down here you can use. Follow me. You'd better not keep the senator waiting."

Spud grunted and followed.

● ● ●

Spud watched as his father eventually appeared on the screen. Despite the senator contacting *him*, his father then made Spud wait 17 minutes until he actually took the call. By the time his father appeared on screen, Spud was sitting back in his chair, feet up and crossed over on the desk, hands behind his head.

"You always answer a transmission like that?" Senator Whitlam greeted him, his always-appraising eyes piercing through the screen. He was seated at the desk in his home office with a backdrop of a shelf of awards and prestige photos with a who's who of politics, sport and entertainment. As usual he was dressed impeccably, his peppered hair smooth and styled. Even his mustache was trimmed in a perfectly straight line.

Spud slowly lowered his feet and sat up straighter. "Only when I have to wait *hours* for someone to show up. *You* called me, remember?"

"It was ten minutes. Another call came in that I had to take."

"Yeah, and I'm glad to see you're alive too, Dad. Thanks for enquiring about my health after I was nearly," Spud paused, wondering how much his father knew, "killed."

"I heard. You stole a black ops weapon and several people died."

"I didn't steal it. My *ex* stole it and dropped me in the shit."

"Perhaps you should reconsider the types of people you associate with."

"Well, she's dead now. The navy blew her up in my escape pod, so no problems there," he said plainly, then swallowed the guilt he felt as it stung more than he thought it would. As much as he hated Shayla after what she did, he still wouldn't have wished death upon her.

His father eyed him for a moment. "What about your crew?"

"What about them?"

"Are you going to disassociate yourself from them when this is over? They're all military drop-outs."

"So am I."

"You were medically discharged. They weren't. I've looked at their files. They're questionable and littered with infractions and disciplinary actions."

"Yeah, well, those questionable ex-soldiers are my friends," Spud said, making sure to eye his father as directly as he could over the transmission screen, "my *family*."

"No, your *family* is on his way to you. Tim will be there within the hour."

"Why'd you send him?"

"You should be grateful he's going with you. Tim is our best soldier and *your* best shot of making it through this mission in one piece. Now, I have a meeting to get to. I just wanted to check in with you—"

"So you can let me know how disappointed you are with me once again?"

His father studied him silently for a moment.

"I won't lie," the senator eventually said. "You *have* disappointed me, Spelton. And if the public hear about this? My son, *a thief*?" The senator shook his head. "But if you do this, you will be redeemed, and no one will ever know. You will be someone I can be proud of."

"In the eyes of the public," Spud said. "Someone you can parade around like you do Tim. Someone you can use to win points of favor in the senate."

His father sighed, disappointed. "I'm not here to argue with you. Do this mission, rectify your wrongs... and stay safe. Good luck," he said, then moved to end the transmission.

"Dad?" Spud stopped him.

The senator paused and looked at him.

"You going to let me speak with Mom before I go in?"

"No. You can speak with her after."

"And if I don't make it out? I'd like to speak to her now."

"She's not here. She's on one of her trips. And she has no idea what you're about to do. It'll do neither of you any good to speak. She'll be a mess and she'll make you a mess. And you don't need that before a mission." His father paused, considered Spud a moment. "You always were each other's weak spot. If you wish to speak with her again, then I guess you'd better make it out alive."

His father ended the comms.

Spud sighed heavily. "Thanks for the pep talk."

CHAPTER TWO

Spud walked down the corridor toward the Gabriel's briefing room. He met Grey just outside the door.

"How'd it go?" she asked.

Spud thought for a moment. "I think I'd rather face five Pantheras than five of my father."

"Ouch. That good, huh?"

He nodded, and they entered the room.

Inside stood the stocky Admiral Eames, his balding Chief Science Officer, Lieutenant Carlton, and the lean medical officer, Dr. Jeavors, who had overseen the care of Spud and his crew. They barely had time to greet each other, before the door opened again and everyone in the room paused to watch, in awe, those who entered.

Major Timothy "Tiberius" Whitlam entered with an air of celebrity clinging to him. It had been a couple of years since Spud had seen his older brother and time had been kind to him. He was 6'1, broad-shouldered, and, hell, even handsome with his angular features, blue eyes and short, thick brown hair. He looked nothing like Spud, who was shorter than his brother, stockier, blond-haired and brown-eyed. Tiberius looked like their father, while Spud looked more like their mother.

Tiberius came to a stop as his team spilled around him. Seven in total, with one woman and six men, they were dressed in their finest navy-blue Galactic Force combat fatigues, each echoing the confidence of their leader. The admiral stepped forward and formal greetings were made before Tiberius broke into a smile and they hugged and patted each other's back. Everyone, even the admiral, loved his brother.

It took a few moments of more introductions of the team to the Gabriel's officers before Tiberius' eyes moved farther afield and landed on Spud. He paused a moment, and Spud thought he saw his brother's face soften briefly, before taking on that confident grin again and approaching.

"Little brother," his deep voice boomed. "It's been a while."

"It has," Spud nodded. Tim was three years older than Spud, but often acted like he was ten years older.

"I see you're back in uniform," Tiberius cast his eyes over him.

"It's temporary."

"Got yourself in some trouble, I see."

"Yeah, but it's okay, because my big brother just flew in to save the day, so," Spud shrugged, "what's to worry about, huh?"

Tiberius' eyes twinkled at the barb, before he turned around and gestured to his team. "Not just me. You got the best damn team in the universe at your disposal. We're here and we're ready to kill some feral cats."

"Big-ass feral cats," Nikita corrected him.

"Not cats. Jaguars. But bigger," Glossy folded her heavily tattooed arms, "with camouflage like you've never seen before."

"And they're fast," Grey said. "And incredibly strong and smart."

"And they've got venom in their claws," Finn added.

"About that..." Jeavors spoke up while also motioning with his lean arms for people to take seats around the briefing table. "We have good news for the two of you who received the claw wounds and who've been given the anti-venom treatment."

"Good news?" Spud asked, taking a seat at the table alongside Grey and his crew.

"Yes," Jeavors said, as Tiberius' unit took the other side of the briefing table. "We've tested your blood and it seems the anti-venom has inoculated you against further poisoning. Should you receive more claw wounds, you will not be affected by the venom."

Spud and Finn exchanged a glance.

"Well, that's good news," Spud said. "So long as we don't bleed to death from the wounds or have our throats ripped out, we'll be fine."

"The venom protection is not to be sniffed at," Jeavors said firmly.

"Why don't you inoculate all of us?" Tiberius asked.

"Because we don't have time for the anti-venom to work," Jeavors said.

"Why not?" Tiberius asked.

"Because it put us," Spud motioned to Finn and himself, "in a coma for few days."

"So, we delay the op for a few days," Tiberius said.

"We can't," said the admiral. "Bracken-Loti is a highly volcanic planet. The largest of these volcanoes, Grindow's Peak, is showing signs that an eruption could be imminent. We need to clear the planet and get down there so we can do what we can to stabilize things. If it blows, it could spew lava for decades. We can't have that. This volcano sits right beside the largest seam of magnetite that Colonial Ore wish to mine from the planet. They're funding this operation. We need that magnetite for our ships, so it's in our interest to assist them."

"What do you mean by 'stabilize things'?" Grey asked. "You can't stabilize a volcano, sir."

"We believe we can," Carlton, the science officer, answered. "We believe with our technology we can create smaller vents to enable release of the pressure, and we can control the directional flow of any lava, away from the site upon which we plan to mine."

"That sounds like a disaster waiting to happen," Spud said. "Why don't you just let the volcano take care of the Pantheras?"

"Because the damage that would occur, could prevent access to the magnetite. We don't have time," the admiral said. "This goes beyond me. There is a lot of money sitting beneath the soil of Bracken-Loti and a lot of people are applying pressure to get moving. Our job is to clear the Pantheras and any other creature that poses a threat to the incoming human population. Once that's done, we pull out and let the scientists deal with the volcano so the mining companies can take control. This is a step-by-step process, gentlemen, and we are the first step."

"Understood, sir," Tiberius said. "But when you say 'any other creature that poses a threat', is there anything in particular we should know about?"

"The Pantheras were sent down there to clear a rodent infestation," Carlton answered. "The rodents were carnivorous and hunted in packs. They... attacked and killed many of our early mining and scientific settlers, before we pulled them out. We believe the Pantheras have now cleared most of these rodents, but they may not have gotten them all. They may have just scared them away to other areas. They could still pose a risk."

"So how do we find the Pantheras?" Grey asked. "The planet isn't large, but still far too big for our small group to cover."

"What we learned from the settlers, before we lost contact, was that the Pantheras seemed to prefer sticking to the areas of jungle at the foot of Grindow's Peak. This was, initially, where the rodents were found too. But it makes sense, because the jungle provides much easier coverage for the Pantheras to use their camouflage to full effect. So the Pantheras have staked a claim in that territory and we need to take it back."

"So, all we have to do," Spud said sarcastically, "is track down and kill *five* Pantheras, watch out for any remaining killer rodents, and hope the volcano doesn't erupt all over us."

"Well," Carlton said cautiously, "the Pantheras are expensive assets, so we would prefer you to tranq them and box them up for us."

Spud paused a moment, before erupting in laughter. Nikita joined him, as Glossy and Finn smiled. Grey's face, however, was stony.

"Something funny?" Admiral Eames asked.

"Yeah," Spud said. "I'm sorry, sir, but if a Panthera comes for me and I have the choice of using a tranq gun or a real gun, I'm not going for the tranq gun."

"You'll do what I order you to," Tiberius said firmly, shutting down the line of conversation. He looked back at the admiral. "What's the plan going in, sir?"

Carlton worked a console and brought up a holographic map of the green-blue planet that was Bracken-Loti, zooming in on an area away from Grindow's Peak.

"You'll land here," the admiral said, pointing to an open plain. "This was the main drop-off site the settlers used. A day's walk from there you'll find the Hacienda. This is the only shelter you'll find on Bracken-Loti, the only one the settlers managed to build before we lost contact."

"You mean before they all died," Spud said.

Tiberius shot him another look to shut up.

The admiral gave him a similar look, but continued on: "Past the Hacienda it's a half-day walk to reach the start of the jungle. Beyond that, you'll have another several hours walk on the crude paths the settlers managed to clear. Beyond that, it's thick jungle for two days to reach the base of Grindow's Peak."

"'We're dropping traps at various spots, to assist you in capturing them," the science officer said. "If you can lure or flush the Pantheras to the traps, all you need to do is get them inside, close the doors behind them, and the trap will take care of the rest. It'll gas them and knock them out until we decide to wake them up again."

"Yeah," Spud said, "just like the box the last Panthera was in on my ship."

"Which held it fine until your adventures with the Guantano mob forced its opening," Admiral Eames said.

Spud went to say something but stopped when he saw the look of guilt on Grey's face. It had been her team that had opened the box, and she was the only one who'd made it off the *Benobi* alive. He felt the guilt slash at him too. Ultimately, it was his fault for allowing the box on his ship in the first place. She'd just been doing her job. He wanted to tell her that and take her guilt away.

"You'll be equipped with an Eagle-Eye," Carlton said, bringing his attention back, "which will help search for and locate the Pantheras for you."

"So, keep that drone close, and you'll be fine," the admiral said.

Tiberius gave a short sharp nod. "Will do, sir."

"Any questions?" the admiral asked.

Tiberius shook his head, but his second-in-command, a man named Grant with a scarred cheekbone and an LT's rank, sat forward.

"Who'd have thought we'd find ourselves hunting cats and mice?" he said dryly.

Another LT with a peppered crew cut, named Lorenzo, laughed. "Better stock up on the cheese, because we're about to have ourselves a party!"

"Let's fall out and prep for departure!" Tiberius called, then stood and led his eager team out the door.

Spud looked at Grey and his *Benobi* team.

"You're right, Glossy," he said. "We're all going to die."

● ● ●

Spud watched as the room emptied, but he lingered within, his reluctance overwhelming. He eventually stood and moved to the observation window. There in the distance, but growing larger by the minute, was the green-blue orb that was Bracken-Loti. It reminded him a little of Earth, but it looked much, much greener.

"It's kinda beautiful, huh?" Grey's voice sounded behind him. He glanced at her then looked back out the window, nodding. She came up to stand beside him.

"Who would've thought something so beautiful could be so deadly," she said gazing down at the planet.

"Story of my life," Spud said, then gave a smile. "It must be female."

Grey's eyes flashed a look of amusement. "There you go again. You can't blame the entire female population for your poor taste in women."

"I don't," he said. "Besides, I've changed now."

"Yeah?" she said, studying the planet, the green-blue hues lighting her features.

"Yeah. My taste in women has improved. *Dramatically.*"

She looked at him and they held each other's gaze for a moment, before she gave her attention to the planet again.

"It's a shame you're convinced we're all going to die then."

Spud shrugged. "Who knows. Maybe we'll make it out. Maybe we'll get lucky."

"Maybe we *will* get lucky." She threw him another glance.

He eyed her blond curly hair, tied back in its bun, her green eyes reflecting the vision before her. He looked down at the planet, thought for a moment, then looked back at her. "If we do make it out... what would you say to having dinner with me sometime?"

Grey looked at him. "Dinner?"

Spud nodded.

"As in a date?" she asked. "You're asking me out on a date?"

"Yeah. Call it a dying man's wish."

Grey turned her body toward him. "A dying man's wish... Well, Spud, I gotta say, I hate a man who promises something and then doesn't deliver. So, if you're asking me out on a date, that means you'd better deliver. If you stand me up, I'm going to be pissed."

Spud turned his body toward hers. "So, is that a yes?"

Grey stared at him with a twinkle in her eyes. "I like dinner."

"So do I."

She studied him. "And I *especially* like dessert."

"Dessert?" Spud said. "I like dessert too... *A lot.*"

"Well, then. If we make it out of there, you can take me to dinner." She stepped closer to him. "And if you play your cards right, maybe we'll even have dessert."

Spud's eyes flooded with warmth. "Dinner *and* dessert. Now there's a hell of a good reason to pull my ass off that planet alive."

"Isn't it?" she smiled.

Her eyes poured warmth into his for a moment, before she turned and walked away. "Let's get ready for departure."

CHAPTER THREE

Spud, dressed in full combat fatigues and armed with his navy-issued dual-fire squad weapon, pistol and bayonet, strapped himself in beside Finn and watched as the rest of the team loaded onto the dropship. Memories of his time as a soldier on the *Katoma* flooded back. Suddenly his uniform felt itchy upon his skin and the large gun in his hand felt heavy – despite how glad he was to have it, knowing where he was going.

Tiberius was last aboard. He paused in front of Grey and extended his hand.

"We weren't formally introduced. Tim."

Grey looked back at him. "Lieutenant Grey."

He read the name sewn on her breast pocket. "Eve. Nice to meet you, Eve." Tiberius gave a smile before turning to the ten bodies awaiting departure, while

Nikita peered back from the cockpit. "Alright, soldiers! Shit is about to get real." Tiberius extended his hand and projected a hologram of the planet from the data-band around his wrist. "Once again, we will be dropped off here," he pointed to the open field, "then we will hump it north to the Hacienda, that's our base for the night. Following day, we get to laying traps and rounding up those kitty-cats. Make no mistake, though, we are entering dangerous, enemy territory, so keep your wits about you. Everybody test your trackers, one last time."

Everyone activated their data-bands. All the bodies on the ship appeared as little red blips on Tiberius' holographic map.

"Good. Byron?" Tiberius said, looking over at his only female soldier, an athletic black woman with a sergeant's rank. "Is the Eagle working and stowed?"

"Yes, sir," she replied, "pre-checks done and it's ready to soar."

"Good," Tiberius said, looking around at his soldiers again. "Now if we stick together, we'll have plenty of eyes on our six to clean up those bastards if they come at our backs. They are fast, they are strong, they are deadly," Tiberius stared each and every one of them in the eye with all seriousness before finally cracking a smile. "But so are we. So, mount up motherfuckers. Let's go kick some ass!"

A chorus of "Yeah!", "Right on!", "Don't you know it!" broke out in response, hands were slapped, and laughter erupted. Spud looked at Finn, seated beside him, then Grey, then Glossy. They were in no celebratory mood.

Tiberius looked to Nikita. "Start the engines, pilot. Let's hit the road."

Nikita exchanged a glance with Spud, then turned back to the flight desk.

Spud exhaled and closed his eyes. "Just think of dessert... Just think of dessert."

"Dessert?" Finn asked.

"Nothing," Spud said, opening his eyes. He felt the engines start and the ship begin to move toward the *Gabriel*'s hangar bay exit. He heard and felt the engines rev higher, felt the jerk of fast forward movement, before bright light engulfed them and daylight poured in through the observation windows.

A black corporal named Jones raised his arms in the air and hollered, as Spud felt a surge of butterflies in his gut. Nikita had literally dropped the ship from the *Gabriel*, and the sudden falling sensation made Spud's stomach jump into his throat. He should be well used to it by now, but he realized that this time things were different. Knowing his destination, and his enemy, had him on edge.

The rest of Tiberius' team joined in whooping and cheering, enjoying the ride. For some, it was through pure ignorance—they had no real idea of what they were about to face. But he knew for the rest it would be a way to burn off excess nervous energy. False bravado was a thing. No one wanted to go on a mission with soldiers second-guessing their abilities. They had to *believe* they were about to kick some ass.

Spud didn't need to get his heart pumping faster. The anxiety and the adrenaline rush from what they were about to do was enough. Barely a week ago he'd fought one Panthera and scarcely survived. He was not looking forward to now facing five.

He glanced over at his brother. Tiberius was focused,

not whooping and hollering like his team, though his face did bear the slightest of smiles for the carry on. He was their leader. It was his job to be the calm, steady, confident one, and Tiberius had the role down pat.

As soon as the ship leveled out, Jones shouted, "Let's get the party started, Tiberius!"

Tiberius smirked and reached above his head to the comms panel and suddenly music was blaring through the speakers. More whooping and hollering sounded, barely audible over the deafening music.

Spud's heart rate shot up another notch.

He quickly unbuckled, marched over to the comms panel and shut it off.

"Hey, man," Jones yelled with a furrowed brow.

"Keep it off," Spud hissed through gritted teeth to Tiberius.

"What the hell you think you're doing?" Lorenzo unbuckled and approached him.

Tiberius held out his hand to stop Lorenzo.

"What's your problem?" Tiberius asked Spud.

"My problem is that the Pantheras hate noise. So, if we land blaring that shit across the planet, we might as well be ringing the goddamn dinner bell. They will come and they will cut us down as soon as we exit the ship. Anything to stop the noise!"

"Is that so?" Tiberius said.

"Yes!"

"That's yes, *sir*, young Whitlam," the LT, Grant, said, taking the other side of Spud to Lorenzo and fixing his square shoulders and jaw. "Show some respect."

"Actually, I go by the name Compton," Spud corrected him. He looked back at Tiberius. "You might be in charge of this mission, but we know what the

Pantheras can do. So, you show *us* some respect."

He held Tiberius' stare a moment longer, then squeezed past Lorenzo, went back to his seat and buckled in, avoiding the glances he was getting from Finn and Grey.

Tiberius looked around at his team unphased by the outburst. "If the *experts* say silence, then silence it is."

● ● ●

"We're approaching the drop-off point," Nikita's voice sounded over the speakers in back.

"Roger that," Tiberius spoke into his comms. "Get ready, people!"

Tiberius extended his arm and engaged his data-band. A hologram projected, showing the footage from the ship's external cameras. They were approaching a clearing surrounded by tall trees with dark, waxy leaves.

"We won't have long," Tiberius called out. "Once the Eagle-Eye is up, we head to the tree line as fast as we can, watching everyone's six. Got it?"

"Copy that!" bellowed Grant as heads erupted into nods of agreement.

Tiberius looked over at Spud. "We'll take the front and rear. Make sure your team stays somewhere in the middle."

"Only Grey and I are going in," Spud said.

"What?" Finn said, as both he and Glossy looked at him.

"You stay and guard the ship," Spud said. "Get ready for an evac."

"No way, man," Finn shook his head.

"Finn, we need bodies here. We need backup—"

"You saved my life on the *Benobi*," Finn spoke over him. "I'm coming to save yours now."

"Finn—"

"I was special forces, Spud. Black ops. I'm more qualified than you to go out there right now."

Spud struggled to find a valid argument to counter that.

"You hired me as your security," Finn said. "So that's what I'm doing. My job."

"We could use as many hands out there as we can get," Grey told Spud.

He sighed and looked back at Finn. "Alright."

"When you two lover boys are finished..." Grant said, bored.

Spud and Finn threw him unaffected glances before Spud looked back at Glossy. "Not you, though, Glossy."

"Are you sure?" she asked.

He gave a firm nod. "You stay here with Nikita and be ready to get us out of there when we need it. Got it? You're our backup."

She gave a nod, as her eyes shone. She reached out her fist and Spud knocked it with his own. "Just say the word, brother," she said. "We'll come get you."

"You'd better," Tiberius said, unbuckling. "Now, shall we?"

They felt the ship kiss the ground with a small bump. Nikita was a smooth operator, and she was doing her best to be as quiet and gentle as she could with the bird. Everyone in back was a flurry of unbuckling, checking their weapons and lining up at the door, ready to make a run for it.

"Release the Eagle-Eye!" Tiberius ordered.

Byron opened a metallic box and pulled out the rounded, metallic drone. It was a standard navy issue, equipped with radar and other scanning functionality, along with basic onboard weaponry. She moved to a compartment in the dropship's hull and opened it, revealing an outer window, and released the Eagle-Eye. Outside, the drone began to circle the ship, climbing higher and higher into the air as it did, scanning their surrounds.

Tiberius watched carefully through his data-band hologram showing the drone's point of view, along with scrolling atmospheric data. Spud scanned the readings, comfortable the oxygen was good and toxins low. Seeing the field was clear and that no Pantheras had been detected, Tiberius closed the hologram down.

"Lorenzo! Foster!" Tiberius called, "get in back! Grant and Byron, you lead. Jones and Heiko, you're with me." He glanced at Spud. "We'll cover the experts."

Spud said nothing, but gripped his weapon tight. He locked eyes with Finn, then with Grey, then he took a deep breath and looked ahead to the rear door of the ship as it slowly yawned open.

As the bright sunlight filtered in, Spud slid on his broad, protective military shades, and began to shuffle quickly to the exit with the team. Lorenzo and the thin-faced Foster moved to crouch either side of the door, weapons scanning the perimeter, as Grant and Byron filed carefully down the gangway to the ground.

Grant and Byron took position either side of the gangway and scanned opposite sides of the clearing. Indicating all-clear, Tiberius led everyone else down onto the planet's surface. He motioned for Jones and

Heiko to take over from Grant and Byron, who swiftly moved for the cover of the tree line.

Spud watched, breathing heavily, scanning the perimeter. It was warm and muggy, equatorial, and he could feel the sweat already building on his brow. He couldn't help but wonder what a camouflaged X03 would look like in these conditions.

Grant and Byron made the tree line safely. Tiberius motioned for Finn and Grey to move with him toward the tree line next. Spud watched them move fast and low and held his breath until he saw them hit their destination. Jones tapped Spud on the shoulder and motioned for him to follow as they went next, moving fast and low with the stocky sergeant named Heiko, to reach the other group. Lieutenant Lorenzo and Corporal Foster soon joined them, then they all watched as the dropship's mouth closed.

Spud took a moment to view the ship and its perimeter, grateful that Nikita and Glossy were safe for now. Then he turned and began to make his silent way through the shadowy trees, following Tiberius' team.

CHAPTER FOUR

They moved slowly, quietly, through the flora of Bracken-Loti. Spud's lenses had automatically lightened to adjust for his darkened surroundings. He blinked his eyes to clear them. He was scanning so intently for any Panthera's camouflage that every now and then he remembered he hadn't blinked in some time and his eyes were dry.

The exotic forest was filled with all manner of strange plants and growths. From a distance they looked earthly, but on closer inspection it was clear they were not. The shrubs and flowers and leaves of trees held patterns, and even hues, of green that he was sure he'd never seen before.

"Wait. Spud, stop." Nikita's voice came through the comms piece in his ear. She'd been following them through their lenses, seeing what they were seeing. "That plant to your left, Spud."

Spud turned his body and reached out with his gloved hand toward a yellowy-green shrub with perfectly triangular leaves, ingrained with perfectly angular veins.

"Don't touch it!" Nikita hissed.

"Why not?" Spud asked, retracting his hand.

"Because according to the little guidebook on Bracken-Loti the admiral gave us, that bitch is poisonous as fuck. Stay away from it. Says here it's covered in an acid resin that will eat right through those gloves and into your skin."

"Great," Sergeant Heiko said nearby. "Now we gotta watch out for the plants too."

"Less talk, more walk," Tiberius said. "Don't touch the plants."

They continued on, Spud's attention occasionally distracted by the Eagle-Eye circling overhead in between the trees. It seemed to form a regular search pattern, but every now and then it would suddenly veer off in a particular direction and circle other spots. That made Spud nervous. What did it see that they could not?

"How much further to the Hacienda?" Corporal Foster asked. Spud noticed the sweat shining on the young man's pale brow.

"Twenty-five klicks," Tiberius answered. "You thinking 'bout dinner already, Fos?"

"I'm always thinking about dinner, sir."

"I'm gonna eat me a horse worth tonight," Jones chimed in.

"Ain't no horses here, Jonesy," Byron said. "But it's nice of you to offer to cook dinner for everyone."

"Cooking's a pink job, isn't it?" Jones grinned.

Byron paused and turned her weapon toward him. Jones laughed, then went to move on, but ran into Grey who also stood there, an immovable wall, staring at him.

"No," Grey said firmly, "I think she said *you* were cooking dinner."

Jones stared back, unsure what to make of her. Byron smirked and kept moving.

Grey, her face a mask, turned and continued forward also.

Tiberius glanced at Spud. "I like her," he smiled, as Grey walked away.

Spud noticed the way Tiberius watched Grey and didn't like it one bit, but he said nothing and moved on.

● ● ●

They continued carefully for another few hours, which was thankfully uneventful. Spud noticed the trees becoming sparser and the ground growth thicker, indicating more sunlight passing through the canopy, and hence they were approaching another clearing.

"Must be closing in on the Hacienda soon," Finn said, a few meters to Spud's right.

He nodded and scanned their surrounds again. Grant and Byron were out front; Jones, Heiko and Tiberius were spread out equal distance apart in a line behind them. Spud, Finn and Grey were next, with Lorenzo and Foster behind.

As the clearing came into view in the near distance, it captured Spud's attention. The sunlight was entrancing. He couldn't wait to get away from all these plants and what might be hiding underneath.

As if on cue, something scuttled nearby, moving with lightning speed. Everyone swung their weapons toward the sound.

"What the hell was that?" Foster asked.

"Quiet!" Grant hissed.

They stood in silence, the sweeping of their weapons the only movement.

"It was too small to be a Panthera," Spud said. "Trust me."

The soldiers threw him a curious glance.

"Keep moving," Tiberius ordered. "Keep your eyes open. Whatever it was, if it comes ag—"

The creature bolted again. It looked like some kind of leathery goat. Foster fired at it and Jones joined in too. The sound of their gunfire rang through the air. Spud shot a nervous look at Finn, then charged at them both.

"Cease fire! Cease fire!" Spud hissed.

Lorenzo stepped up, aimed and fired. He hit his target. The creature cried out and collapsed.

"It's not a Panthera!" Spud spat at Tiberius. "But now, thanks to that racket, they might just know where we are!"

"Well, it's our job to find them," Lorenzo said plainly.

"But how about we find them when one of those traps are nearby, huh?" Spud said.

Tiberius walked past Spud to the dying creature. They all moved in for a look, keeping an eye on their surrounds. The creature was a little larger than a goat, and leathery like a crocodile, its body covered in razor-sharp horns.

"It's looks like a little fucking dinosaur," Jones said.

"I'm getting a photo of that shit," Foster grinned, holding up his data-band and snapping away.

"Congratulations," Spud said sarcastically to Lorenzo, "you killed a Bracken-Loti goat. That thing would've eaten us where we stood."

"Hey look, pal," Lorenzo stepped toward him, but Finn stepped in front of Spud.

"Back off," Finn warned Lorenzo.

"You back off," Tiberius stepped up to him. "What's done is done." He locked eyes with Spud, then turned to Foster. "You're so enamored with it, you can drag this thing to the Hacienda."

"Why?" Foster asked. "You think we can eat it?"

"I want a closer look at it," Tiberius said. "Move." He looked back at Spud. "All of you."

Foster grabbed the animal's leg and grunted as he heaved it along behind him, while the others continued forward, sweeping their surrounds. Spud didn't move, though. He stood and glared daggers into his brother's back.

Tiberius seemed to sense it. He paused and turned around. "I gave an order, *Compton*."

"Come on," Finn nudged his shoulder. "Let's get to the Hacienda."

Finn moved past him and Spud looked further ahead to Grey, who motioned with her head for him to hurry up.

"Think of dessert," he muttered under his breath. "Just think of dessert."

● ● ●

Within thirty minutes they reached the Hacienda. Built from felled trees, it looked like any old log cabin back on earth. They approached it carefully, Tiberius leading half his team toward it, while the others remained within the tree line.

Spud watched Tiberius' team carefully, glancing around intermittently to the surrounding tree line; the smell of jungle, of dirt and trees, hung in the muggy air around him. Tiberius' team reached the structure with no trouble and entered in a two-by-two formation to clear it. Within moments, Grant reappeared and waved the rest of them forward, then he tapped at his data-band, bringing the Eagle-Eye to the ground, scooped it up and took it inside.

Spud crossed the clearing with the second team and entered the Hacienda to see the inside was rather homely. There was a rough kitchen and fireplace with drying herbs, open paper journals that someone had been writing in, even clothing hanging on a makeshift line to dry.

"How long ago did they say they lost contact?" Heiko asked. "This looks lived in."

"What gave it away?" Byron asked sarcastically. "The burning fire?"

Tiberius ignored them, looking around curiously.

Byron peered into a small closet just inside the door, screwing up her nose. "What *the hell* is that smell?" She closed the door again, revealing a man standing just outside the front door.

Byron, and Spud himself, jumped in fright, as the man, grey-haired, yellow-skinned, and disheveled in appearance, gave a grimy smile.

"That smell," he said in a craggy voice, "is called survival."

CHAPTER FIVE

Grant stepped forward as they turned their guns on the man.

"Who the fuck are you?" Grant demanded.

"Not a Panthera!" Spud said, pushing the muzzle of Grant's gun down.

"No," the man said, "I'm not. And you're in my house, uninvited."

"*Your* house?" Tiberius said, stepping forward. "This belongs to Colonial Ore, I believe."

"Colonial Ore *and* the Assembly of Inter-Planetary Scientists, actually," the man corrected him. "Of which I am a member. This was and always has been a joint venture."

"We thought you were dead," Tiberius said. "They

lost contact with you."

"Yes, they did. But as you can see, I'm fine. Thanks for stopping by." The man motioned them to leave his house.

"Oh, he's *loco*..." Lorenzo muttered.

"Well," Tiberius said, eyeing the man over, analyzing his physical state, wrinkling his nose at the putrid, acidic smell, "we're here now. What say we stay for a chat, maybe get you some medical attention."

"I don't need medical attention. And I'd rather you leave."

"Your skin is yellow," Tiberius said, "that's not normal."

"My skin is yellow because I'm covered in klauten piss."

"Yeah," Byron nodded, looking at the man like he was crazy, "maybe you should come inside and sit down, huh?"

The man stepped inside and Spud nearly gagged at the odor emanating from him as he passed.

"I said I don't need your help," the man said, turning around to them, "and I'd rather you leave. *Now*."

"Why?" Tiberius asked.

"Because you're *not* covered in klauten piss, which means the second the Panthera-X03s get a whiff of your scent and decide there's a new threat to their territory, they'll be on my doorstep. You are bringing danger to all that I've worked for."

"So klauten piss deters the Pantheras?" Spud asked.

"Yes. The klautens are the only animal the Pantheras avoid. It's their horns you see. The Pantheras can't attack them without getting all cut up. A defense mechanism of the klautens is to spray piss when under threat. The Pantheras have learned to avoid the klauten's scent."

"You survived this whole time by covering yourself in piss?" Finn asked.

"Yes," the man nodded. "So, if you would please leave."

"Do you have enough piss for us?" Spud asked.

The man looked at him, part curious, part concerned. "Why? What are you here to do?"

"Rescue you, for one," Tiberius answered. "We have a dropship waiting for us a day's walk away."

"I'm not leaving," the man shook his head, and moved toward the fireplace. He checked there was water in his kettle and hung it over the heat to boil.

"You're not safe here," Tiberius said.

"No, *you're* not safe here. I've been doing just fine."

"I'm not so sure about that," Byron said, holding her nose.

"Why are you here?" the man demanded of Tiberius.

"We're here to remove the Pantheras."

The man stared at him a moment, then gave a rough and ragged laugh. "Why? Has Colonial Ore finally realized the error of their ways?"

"The Pantheras have done their job clearing the rodents, now they're a problem to be removed."

"Give me a break!" the man said bitterly.

"What's your name?" Tiberius asked.

The man muttered something incomprehensible and shook his head as he made his tea.

"Dr. Phineas McLaren," Nikita's voice sounded over their comms. "He's listed in the settler files. He was the chief science officer sent there."

"Dr. McLaren," Tiberius said to the man, who looked

up surprised. His surprise quickly turned into anger.

"Someone watching and listening on your comms, eh? Well, you tell them that I'm not leaving! My work here isn't done. This, *here*, is a beautifully rich ecosystem that we *fucked* with, and now I'm trying to right it!"

"We'll clear the Pantheras," Tiberius said. "Things will return to normal."

"And then what?" McLaren accused. "Colonial Ore will come in here and start digging great holes in the ground, clearing the land, killing the rest of the native fauna and flora?"

"That's not for us to decide," Tiberius said.

"Isn't it?" McLaren stepped up to Tiberius. "I've seen the damage we've done. We introduced just *five* Pantheras, and within weeks they had decimated the local fauna. And you know what happened then? The fauna stopped eating the flora, the plants started to take over, bit by bit, piece by piece, the chain reaction had begun. And this planet will never be the same again. I told them introducing a new species to an enclosed, protected ecosystem would be disastrous, but would they listen? Would they look upon centuries of proof to this fact? When has introducing a new species to any ecosystem ever turned out well? Never!"

"I understand what you're saying, Dr. McLaren," Tiberius said, "but we have our orders. We're here to remove the Pantheras. You can return with us, or you can stay here, I'm not going to force you. But you *will* lend your assistance to us, and you will not get in our way."

"Is that so?" the crusty old man growled.

Tiberius stared down at him, unphased. "Yes. Sir."

McLaren stepped back and glared around at all of them. "I suppose you want to commandeer all my piss stock, hmm? Do you know how hard that stuff is to procure?" He motioned out the door. "And now I've got one less klauten to extract it from thanks to you trigger-happy idiots!"

"Do you ever see Pantheras around here?" Finn asked.

The man eyed him. "You rarely *see* the X03s."

"But do they dwell in these parts?" Spud asked.

McLaren turned his disdain to Spud. "Not for a while. They've learnt this house stinks of klauten piss, so they stay away. But now you're here, who's to say."

"How much stock do you have on hand?" Tiberius asked.

The man hesitated before answering: "I'll have enough to cover some of you. Not all."

Tiberius considered this. "We'll take what you can spare in the morning when we set out for the jungle proper. Tonight, we'll take our chances."

● ● ●

Despite the shelter of the Hacienda, they decided to set the Eagle aloft again. Thankfully, there had been no signs of any threats, and they ate dinner in peace. The damned klauten was hard to crack open with all those horns and leathery skin, but McLaren had it down to a fine art. The meat was terrible, though. Tough as the leather that covered it and more like trying to eat a slab of jerky. Spud ended up spitting his out—and swiftly received a slap over the head from McLaren for needing to waste more klauten piss to cover it.

To make matters worse, Spud had to sit there, watching, while Tiberius turned on the charm, chatting with Grey about their common time patrolling The Wastelands. Finn came and sat down beside him. Spud saw him briefly glance over at Tiberius and Grey.

"Your brother is quite the all-rounder, isn't he?" Finn said quietly.

"Yeah, he's a PR dream," Spud said.

"A hit with the ladies too, by the looks of it."

Spud studied Tiberius. "Nah. He's not her type."

"Oh, yeah? And what's her type?" Finn said, unable to stop the smile sliding up his cheeks. Spud gave him a questioning look.

"You snooze, you lose, Spud," Finn said quietly. "And if I were you, I wouldn't go to sleep while Tiberius is around."

Spud looked over at Tiberius and Grey, then darted his eyes to McLaren, sitting at his desk reading over his notes. Foster and Grant were already asleep. Lorenzo and Byron were just rolling out their packs for sleep, while Heiko and Jones were on lookout with the Eagle-Eye.

Spud checked the time on his data-band, then looked at Tiberius. "Hey, Tim? What say we take the next watch?"

His brother looked at him curiously, then gave a nod. "Alright."

● ● ●

They moved outside to relieve Heiko and Jones, who were more than happy to disappear back inside the

Hacienda.

"So..." Spud said, walking away from the Hacienda, checking the darkened tree line in the distance that surrounded them.

"So," Tiberius said, eyeing him up and down. "Never thought I'd see you back in uniform."

"Neither did I." Spud eyed him. "What with my medical discharge and all that."

"How *is* the leg?" Tiberius said, turning his eyes to scan the distance.

Spud gave a laugh. "Well, the bullet left a nasty scar, but it got me out, I suppose."

"That it did," Tiberius said.

Spud studied him a moment. "Why are you here?" he asked, unable to hide his curiosity any longer.

Tiberius glanced at him, then looked back to their perimeter. "Why do you think?"

"I don't need your protection, Tim."

"Don't you?"

"And if you and dad think this'll pull me back in—"

Tiberius looked back at him. "You think I'm here to pull you back in? I was the one who helped you get out, remember?"

"Yeah, by shooting me in the leg. Thanks for that."

"Hey, it got you out," Tiberius shrugged, still scanning the tree line. "You didn't want to be there and that's a dangerous soldier to have around. If you didn't get yourself killed you were going to get someone else killed."

"So my big brother shot me!"

"Oh, poor little Spelton, picked on again."

Spud shook his head. "I'm sick of fighting with you."

"You think I enjoy this?" Tiberius looked at him. "You

think I enjoy trying to help you all the time and have it constantly thrown back in my face?"

"I never asked for your help."

"No, but you needed it!" Tiberius bit back.

"You're not here to help me out, Tim, you're here to play hero and show Dad why you're his favorite son."

Tiberius' eyes threw daggers at him.

"Am I wrong?" Spud asked.

Tiberius shook his head like Spud was missing the point.

"Just—" Spud bit his tongue on what he was going to say, then he relented and let it go anyway. "Just stay away from my crew, alright? We don't need you."

"You barely survived *one* of those things, now you're going to stand there and tell me you don't need my unit?" Tiberius shook his head again. "You always were a little brat, Spel. Mom spoiled you. Wrapped you up in cotton wool."

"Is that what this is about? Being Dad's favorite wasn't enough, you wanted to be Mom's too?"

Tiberius threw him another sharp look. Spud could tell his brother was now biting his tongue on something.

"How's she doing anyway?" Spud asked. "I never got to speak to her."

"Mom's off on one of her secret hippy holidays apparently."

"Is it just me or is she spending more time away from him lately?"

Tiberius shrugged. "She's always home for formal occasions."

"In front of the cameras," Spud nods. "Dad never did stop working. I'd be bored too."

They threw each other a shared look of

understanding of their parents' complicated marriage.

"So," Spud said, "you seeing anybody?"

"Nope. You?"

Spud hesitated. "Not just yet."

"Not just yet? What does that mean?"

"Nothing."

"Say, is Lieutenant Grey single?"

Spud looked at him. Tiberius met his eye.

"I like her," he smiled.

"Yeah, well," Spud said, "don't go there."

"Why not?"

"Because."

"Because why?"

Spud hesitated. "Because I said."

"I don't see a ring on her finger."

Spud shot him a look of warning and Tiberius grinned.

"Oh, I get it," he said. "You and her, huh?"

Spud turned back to scan the perimeter.

"So, how long that been going on for?" Tiberius asked.

Spud ignored him.

"Or has it even at all?" his brother pushed, analyzing him.

Spud shot him another warning look.

"Or are you just daydreaming about it?" Tiberius grinned, knocking his arm.

"Look, just don't go there, alright."

"Why not?"

Spud started to walk away.

"So how serious is it?" Tiberius asked. "Have you even sealed the deal yet?"

Spud continued to ignore him.

"Oh, you haven't?" Tiberius chuckled. "Well, that means she's still on the menu, little brother. That's fair game, right there."

Spud gave him a hard look. "No. She's not!"

Grey suddenly came charging out of the Hacienda. She bent down scooped up a rock and threw it at Spud.

"Whoa!" he ducked, as another one came flying at Tiberius, who also stepped out of the way. Laughter broke out inside the cabin and they saw faces peering out the windows.

"We can hear you!" Grey hissed angrily, pointing to the Eagle-Eye.

Spud looked up, saw it hovering overhead, then looked back at the cabin. The soldiers were belly-laughing hard, as Grey stormed back inside slamming the door.

Tiberius looked at his soldiers. "Alright, who was it?"

"It was Jones, sir," Byron pointed to the corporal in hysterics. "He tapped into the mic feed."

Tiberius shook his head at them, fighting the smile on his face.

"Shit..." Spud exhaled. He looked at Tiberius. "Thanks for that. Thanks a lot."

He turned and walked off to the other side of the cabin.

CHAPTER SIX

The next morning things were awkward to say the least. Grey avoided Spud and Tiberius at all costs. He could literally see the steam pouring from her ears. If he went anywhere near her, he was sure she would punch him in the face.

If that wasn't bad enough, the sniggers and smiles from Tiberius' soldiers made it worse. Finn said nothing. He just clapped his hand on Spud's shoulder and gave a sympathetic smile as he passed. McLaren, a pair of reading glasses perched on the end of his nose, studied Spud as though he was part of the Bracken-Loti fauna. All the while Tiberius acted like nothing happened.

"So, who's using my piss stock then?" McLaren asked,

resentment clear in his voice. "I can spare enough for two of you."

"Only two?" Jones asked.

"My apologies," McLaren said sarcastically. "If I knew ten soldiers would turn up at my door, I would've procured more."

Tiberius looked around at his team. "Byron and Grey."

"What?" Byron asked.

"You get the piss. Move."

"What? No," Byron said, then added, "Sir."

Tiberius looked at her. "I gave you an order." Byron stepped up to him, lowering her voice, but Spud heard her just fine.

"Sir, no. You give it to one of the others or you draw straws."

"Byron—" Tiberius started to object, but Byron cut him off.

"You make me take it, then you are making me look weak to the team, sir. You are saying to them that I am a woman and I need extra protection that they don't." She stepped closer to him. "I don't, sir. I have more experience than Foster or Jones. Give it them."

"She's right," Grey said, stepping up to them. "And I won't take it either. Give it to the weakest links or draw straws. That's the only way we'll have it."

Tiberius sighed. "Alright, alright. You want to take this moment to stand for women's liberation, I'll give it to you." He looked over at Spud. "You and Finn take it."

"What?" Finn asked.

"You're ex-military, you haven't served for years. You're technically civilians. You get the piss."

"I was black ops," Finn said. "Time may have passed,

but my guess is I'll fare better than your corporals."

"Oh, for fuck's sake!" McLaren said. He dipped a paintbrush in the bucket of klauten piss and slapped it on Finn's back.

"What the hell are you doing?" Finn said, spinning around.

"All this macho bullshit ends here," McLaren said, slapping the brush across Finn's chest. Finn stepped backward from the man, face screwed up at the smell.

"I'm already immune to the venom! I already have protection that they don't."

"Yeah? And from the jaws and claws?" McLaren said. "They'll slice through you like paper, boy!"

"They already have!" he said.

"Enough!" Tiberius said, as Finn backed into him. He pushed Spud's crewman away. "You're it whether you like it or not. Spud, you're next."

Spud looked to Grey. She turned away.

"Give it to one of your corporals," he told his brother, while McLaren continued to slop the putrid yellow piss over Finn, who dry-retched as he did.

Tiberius didn't answer but motioned to Lorenzo and Jones. They approached Spud and he stiffened.

"Really, Tim?" he said. "You're going to force me?"

"No," McLaren said, approaching with piss-saturated brush, "I am."

The soldiers swooped, but Spud quickly sidestepped and pivoted out of the way. McLaren slopped the brush over Lorenzo.

"Ah, shit!" Lorenzo said, holding his hands out, away from the cloudy substance.

"Oh, well," McLaren said, "you're the lucky candidate." He continued sloshing the liquid over

Lorenzo, who screwed up his face, looking to Tiberius.

Tiberius approached Spud. "Really? You're going to be *this* stubborn to prove what a tough guy you are."

"Look who's talking," Spud said.

Tiberius shook his head. "You're going to get yourself killed. Or the rest of us."

Lorenzo was now gagging at the smell he was being pasted with.

"You'll thank me for it, soldier," McLaren told him.

● ● ●

They repacked their supplies and began to file out of the Hacienda, ready to start the day trekking into the jungle proper.

"We hope to be done in a few days," Tiberius said to McLaren. "Once we are, we'll be back this way. You have until then to decide if you're coming home with us."

"You sound so confident that you'll be back," McLaren said, studying him over the top of his glasses.

Tiberius paused, staring at him. "We will be."

"You have no idea what's out there."

"So why don't you put your money where your mouth is, old man," Lorenzo said. "Come with us. Show us the ropes."

"No, thank you. I choose to live."

With that, McLaren went back inside and closed the door. They all stood there a moment staring at the cabin as McLaren's words hung in the air.

"Don't listen to him," Tiberius said, calmly, confidently. "McLaren never had the training or the firepower we do. Let's move out!"

He turned around and began walking toward the trees.

● ● ●

They made their way slowly toward the tree line of the jungle proper, as the Eagle-Eye overhead watched and scanned their surroundings. It was mid-morning and already a sheen of sweat glistened across their foreheads from the muggy heat. In fact, it was so muggy, Spud could see clouds of condensation hanging in the air between the foliage. He glanced around nervously. The last thing they needed was for anything to hinder their vision, not to mention the fact that the heat was bound to make them smell real nice for the X03s.

Speaking of smell, he glanced over at Finn, walking alongside a few feet away. His crewman carefully eyed the trees, his torso thighs and arms covered with the yellow klauten piss, which had dried into a thick paste, and so far didn't appear to be at risk of being washed away with sweat. Lorenzo, and his stench, took up the rear position, while Spud's brother led the group. Ever the hero.

"What the hell was that?" Jones hissed quietly, swatting the air.

"That's a big ass mosquito!" Foster whispered back, now swatting too.

Spud heard something roaring past his ear. It sounded like a mosquito, except maybe one that was powered by a turbo engine.

"If the Pantheras don't eat us," Grant smiled, "looks like the mosquitos will."

"Actually," Glossy's voice sounded over their comms

along with the tapping of keys, "it's not just the mosquitos. From what past attempts at settling the planet discovered, there's a lot of unfriendly things on this planet. I'd watch your step."

"Well, that's reassuring," Spud muttered.

Tiberius held his hand up for them to stop and checked the data-band on his wrist. Spud saw he was projecting information from the Eagle-Eye. Tiberius tapped at the screen, then Spud watched as the Eagle-Eye moved to scan the first part of the jungle before them.

"Goddamn, it's hot," Jones said, tugging at his shirt.

"Yeah?" Finn said, lifting a clean part of the hem of his shirt to wipe his brow, "try dealing with the klauten stench as well."

"Whoa!" Foster said, staring at the healing claw marks down Finn's chest.

The rest of the team turned to stare too.

"You got that from the Panthera?" Byron asked, as Tiberius looked back curiously.

Finn nodded, lowering his shirt. "Spud, too."

"Show us yours, man," Jones said.

Spud shook his head.

"Go on," Tiberius said, moving toward him. "Show us."

Spud shook his head again, but Tiberius grabbed him and spun him around, lifting his shirt.

"Whoa!" Jones said this time. "They got big-ass claws, huh?"

"That they do," Tiberius said after a moment, lowering Spud's shirt again.

"How'd you know they were on my back?" Spud asked him.

Tiberius looked at him. "Your med told me."

"When did you speak to my med?"

Tiberius ignored him, moving away as he checked his data-band again.

"Eagle-Eye clear," he said. "Let's move on."

Then his brother raised his weapon and stepped carefully into the shadows of the tall trees.

CHAPTER SEVEN

They moved along slowly in the dappled light from above, scanning their surrounds and dripping with sweat as they followed the worn tracks from the settlers that weaved around tree trunks and ground growth, heading deeper into the jungle.

"So where are the animals we're supposed to be wary of?" Heiko asked, noting the lack. "You think the Pantheras have eaten them all?"

"Maybe," Grey said, "or they're just hiding from the new predator in their midst."

A sudden awful screech up high made them tilt their guns aloft. In one of the tall trees sat a family of the most brightly colored parrot-like birds Spud had ever seen. Red, green, blue. And large. *Very* large, with massive black beaks. They looked similar to those found on Earth in South America, but their eyes were blue and their feet similar to those of a monkey, and at the tips of their wings they had hands similar to a human, with fleshy palms and five claw-like fingers.

"Wow. They look like they could eat us," Byron said.

"They'll eat my gun if they try," Foster said.

They moved forward and Spud could see with every step the jungle thickening around them. He didn't like it. There were too many opportunities for the X03s to hide and strike from. They should've waited out in the open and made the Xs come to them. They would've stood a chance then.

"Where are the traps?" Spud asked Tiberius. "I don't see how they'd get the traps down here with all the trees."

Tiberius kept his eyes on their perimeter. "They're located in a number of small clearings, but this is how we get to them. Through the jungle. All the traps are marked out on the map. You can access it on your data-band."

"We're sitting ducks in this jungle."

"Ah, shit," Foster said.

Spud looked back at him and saw the muzzle of his weapon was caught up in some vines. Foster managed to pull it free, a sticky sap stringing between the vine and gun. The soldier continued on a couple of steps before he suddenly tripped over, face first.

"Goddamn. *Stupid*..." Foster cursed himself, sitting up and turning around.

Spud saw him unhooking a vine from his ankle, then heard a rustle overhead and looked up the tree.

The vines were moving.

He looked back to Foster and saw more of them tightening around his ankles.

"Oh, shit," Spud said. "The vines!"

"What?" Jones and Grant paused to watch.

Spud moved to Foster, checked to see the other soldiers had them covered, then hooked his weapon over his shoulder. "They're alive! They're trapping him!"

"Shit!" Foster yelled as more vines encircled him. Heiko and Grant moved to assist but by the time they reached him, the vines were all over Foster. Grant pulled out his bayonet and began hacking at the vines as Spud and Heiko tried to pull Foster free.

But the vines didn't like that.

The green rubbery tendrils began swinging for each of them.

Spud and Heiko swatted them away defensively, pulling their bayonets too.

"Stop moving!" Grant hissed at Foster, who was struggling and making it hard for Grant to free him.

"Get it off me!" Foster was panicking now.

The three men hacked, swatted and pulled at the vines, but Foster was suddenly yanked along the ground away from them.

"Jesus!" Jones said, standing a few meters away from them. "It's taking him!"

"Hurry!" Heiko said, jogging forward and trying to tug Foster back as the soldier shouted in panic. "Get it off me! Get it off me!"

"Just stay calm!" Spud said. "Quiet down!"

Byron and Jones stepped forward now, while Lorenzo, Finn, Grey and Tiberius hung back, eyeing their perimeter.

"Sort that shit out!" Tiberius spat over his shoulder,

checking his data-band.

"Anything?" Spud asked his brother, nervous about the noise as he tugged on the vines and swatted those going for his neck and limbs.

Tiberius shook his head but kept darting his eyes between the band and their surrounds, as he wiped his brow.

"Can the Eagle read us all the way down here with this humidity?" Grey asked. Spud saw she was looking up to the treetops, to the dim shadow overhead of the Eagle-Eye circling.

"It has a ten klick range," Tiberius told her. "That should give us enough warning."

"FUCK!" Foster yelled, grabbing at a vine that had encircled his throat.

"Shut up!" Lorenzo hissed over his shoulder. "Stop ringing the goddamn dinner bell!"

And then Spud heard it. In the distance.

The faint cry of a kitten...

Grey and Finn heard it too and stiffened.

"That was closer than ten klicks," Spud said, dropping the vines and moving back from Foster. He threw his brother a worried glance.

"What is?" Tiberius said, noting the look on his face.

Spud stepped further away from Foster, listening. He heard the *meow* again. Closer.

He pulled his gun off his shoulder and snapped it up.

"That's an X!" he whispered loudly. "That's the sound they make before they attack. It sounds like a kitten!"

"A what?" Jones looked at him, not sure whether to take him seriously.

"It's choking him!" Byron said looking at Foster.

They looked back to Foster whose face was turning

red as he struggled to breathe. The vines suddenly yanked him up off the ground by his feet, dangling him like a catch of the day.

"Jesus!" Grant said, face strained as he tried to pull Foster back down to the ground.

"Fuck this shit!" Jones said, spraying fire up high across the vines.

"Stop it! Shut up!" Spud hissed, as bits of vine blew apart and rained down on them.

Foster's body dropped a little, his head now just off the ground. But then the vines suddenly pulled tighter. Foster gargled in pain.

Then came the barbs.

Like dinosaur teeth they shot out from pores in the vine's surface and punctured Foster's flesh.

He gave a garbled scream as his blood flicked across them all. Thrashing about, the others stepped closer, trying desperately to lend aid. Spud stepped back, however. He knew they were making too much noise. He exchanged an anxious glance with Grey and Finn.

And then they heard it.

The deep guttural growl of a Panthera about to attack.

Like a lightning flash it lunged out of the undergrowth in its mirrorlike camouflaged state.

"Move!" Spud yelled in unison with Grey.

The soldiers didn't see it coming and the Panthera-X03 hit Foster's screaming body with a thud.

The barbs suddenly retracted and the vines retreated up high, as Foster's body fell into full possession of the Panthera.

"Move!" Grey yelled again, desperately wanting to take aim but fearful of hitting the soldiers who stared stunned at the camouflaged creature.

With swift and violent movements, the Panthera yanked Foster's screaming body away from them, knocking Heiko down as it did, and shot back into the undergrowth before they even really knew what had happened.

A barrage of gunfire spat into the shrub after it, before Tiberius' voice cut through the din. "STOP! CEASE FIRE! CEASE FIRE! YOU'LL HIT FOSTER!"

"Did you see that thing?" Jones shook his sweat-sheened face, eyes popping white.

"He won't survive that," Spud said, his voice tinged with shock. "He's dead already."

Tiberius, refusing to believe it, barged into the scrub, gun out front, following the trail of Foster's blood. Grant and Lorenzo moved in close behind him, and the others followed suit.

Finn eyed Spud, panting. "Why did we agree to do this again?"

Spud didn't answer but moved after his brother's soldiers. They couldn't hear Foster anymore, but they did hear a crackle and crunch as the Panthera took a bite of him.

"Jesus!" Heiko shrank back beside Spud.

They heard the growl again and the sound of Foster's body being dragged. They followed the blood.

"He's dead," Lorenzo said, taking aim. "Let's just shoot it."

Tiberius didn't answer, his eyes fixed on the shrubs the sound came from.

"Tibe?" Grant asked, eye fixed to his gun's sight.

"Not until I have visual confirmation that he is dead," Tiberius said quietly. "We do not leave the living to die."

In another flash, the snarl sounded, and the pink-skinned muscled meat flew out at them. In their close quarters, they didn't have time to fire before it had darted swiftly around them—right into the path of Grey.

She'd hung back, waiting. And as the X flew toward her, she put a line of bullets through its torso. The Panthera fell to the ground, skidding, shrieking, spurting blood. Grey moved toward it, continuing to spray the thing with bullets as it tried to run. They watched in shock, or maybe awe, as she did. The seconds ticked past as she unloaded into the creature until it collapsed and no longer moved. Grey watched its lifeless body a few moments more, then finally satisfied it was dead, she looked back at the team, panting.

They continued to stare in silent awe.

"They don't die easy," she explained calmly. "You gotta make *real* sure they're dead."

Tiberius gave her an impressed nod, then swept back into the thick undergrowth to his fallen colleague.

Spud threw Grey a look of relief, then followed his brother to where he crouched beside his dead soldier. Foster was covered in blood, his body pockmarked from the vines; his neck, jaw and shoulder torn open by the Panthera, his head almost decapitated.

"They're no ordinary cats," Spud said quietly, turning his eyes away.

Tiberius looked at him. At first Spud thought he saw shock, but it quickly morphed into a precision focus. He pushed past Spud to study the X's carcass.

No longer in camouflage, the furless, muscled creature lay like a smoking bloody lump of meat. Its pink skin reminding Spud of pictures he'd seen of a kitten fetus inside the womb.

"Man, they're big," Jones said in shock, standing beside him.

"Look at the damn muscles on the thing," Grant said, eyeing it.

"And the camouflage," Lorenzo added. "I barely saw it when it was camouflaged."

"Are they eyes?" Byron asked, face screwed up as she stared at the darkened patches that sat beneath the pink skin where its eyes should be.

Tiberius nodded, his eyes scanning the beast.

"Why didn't your Eagle-Eye pick it up?" Finn asked Tiberius.

Tiberius looked at him, then at the data-band, concerned.

"Must be the camouflage," Spud said. "Something in it traps their heat signature."

Grey nodded. "Between that and the humidity, the Eagle-Eye is useless to us."

"Shit," Byron said tightly. "We got no eyes in the sky?"

"How long can it stay like that?" Tiberius asked. "Camouflaged?"

Spud shook his head. "I don't know."

"What do you mean you don't know?" Tiberius stepped up to him. "You're the expert, right? One of my soldiers just fucking died, so you better be the expert on this and give me some goddamn information!"

"It went in and out on the ship," Spud said. "It was never for long, but that doesn't mean it can't do it for long. I didn't really stop to study the damn thing. I was generally trying to get away from it."

"How *did* you survive trapped on a ship with one of them?" Byron asked.

"Fire," he said. "And some poison. And her," he

motioned to Grey.

She met the stares she received.

"I'm starting to like her a lot," Tiberius said.

Spud threw him a piercing look. A smile twitched briefly at Tiberius' mouth before it disappeared and his face turned hard. "Let's move out. We've got four more out there."

"What about Foster, sir?" Jones asked.

Tiberius looked to where the young man's body lay. He lifted his data-band and projected the map of his soldiers' locator beacons. "We'll collect him on the way back through."

"We could use him as bait," Finn said.

Tiberius' team glared at him.

Finn shrugged. "See if his body draws the others to it."

"What the hell, man?" Jones screwed up his face.

"Let's make them come to us," Finn argued.

"I agree," Spud said.

"We're not using him as bait!" Lorenzo spat.

"You wanna see what else this jungle has to offer?" Spud said. "If the Panthera hadn't killed him, the fucking vines would have!"

"It won't work," Grey said. "They'll smell the body, but they'll also smell us. They'll know it's a trap. Either that, or they'll go for the live bait first. Its instinct is to eliminate threats. We're the bigger threat."

"She's right," Tiberius said. "They'll be drawn to us, regardless. We keep moving."

Spud clicked on his comms. "Nikita?"

"Yeah?"

"Do a sweep and try and find the other four Xs."

"You can't order my ship anywhere," Tiberius said.

"We need to know if they're in the area."

"That's what the Eagle-Eye is for!"

"The Eagle-Eye did shit just then!"

"What makes you think your pilot can do any different?"

"In the ship she's higher off the ground, less of a threat. They may not be camouflaged when they're away from us. She could track them down for us."

"No," Tiberius said, "she preserves fuel cells and gets ready to haul us out of here."

"Tim—"

"I said no!" Tiberius glared at him. "I'm not risking our one ticket out of here." He turned and waved the others forward. "The Eagle-Eye will lead us back to the body when we're done."

Tiberius walked onward and the soldiers moved after their leader, throwing saddened glances at their fallen, butchered comrade as they did.

Finn sighed and looked at Spud. "We could go back?"

"Go back where?" Spud said grumpily. "To jail?" He shook his head and exhaled heavily. "No, we need to follow my goddamn brother."

He reluctantly moved after the other group.

CHAPTER EIGHT

They moved forward, evenly spread, weapons carefully sweeping their surrounds. Although they had been observant before, their focus had now increased tenfold.

Finn tapped Spud on the shoulder and pointed to Heiko who was about five meters in front of them, but off to the side a little. His shoulder and upper arm were covered in what looked like fresh splatters of blood. Spud's face fell and he quickly sped up to walk alongside him.

"Is that Foster's blood? Or did the X's claws scratch you?" he asked.

"It's just a little scratch," Heiko brushed him off. Spud noticed his face looked a little pale and he was panting lightly.

"Tiberius," Spud called, motioning his brother to join them. Tiberius fell back into the group as Grant took over point.

"What is it?" he asked.

"The X scratched him," Spud said. "He's in trouble."

"I'm fine," Heiko protested.

"Now you are," Spud said, as Finn joined them, "but in an hour?"

"It's just a scratch?" Tiberius said looking at it.

"That scratch," Finn said, "is going to turn into the most searing pain you've ever felt. And after that? You're going to fall into a coma. And if you don't get the anti-venom, you'll die."

"They gave me some," Tiberius said, studying Heiko.

"They did?" Spud asked.

Tiberius swung his weapon over his shoulder and pulled a syringe out of his pack.

"What good is that going to do here?" Spud asked. "The anti-venom could still put him into a coma until he stabilizes."

Heiko looked nervously between them. "I'm fine. It's just a scratch, man. I don't know what did it. It was probably one of those vines."

Spud stepped closer to Tiberius. "The anti-venom is useless. He can't go into a coma, Tim. There's no hospital out here. We won't be able to keep him stable."

"I'm fine!" Heiko spat.

Spud turned on his comms. "Nik, we need an evac."

"Roger that. On our way," she replied.

"You don't give the orders around here," Tiberius said, then clicked on his comms. "Evac cancelled. Await my orders."

"What are you doing?" Spud asked.

"I give the orders."

"There's a clearing a few hours northwest from where you are," Nikita said. "We could rendezvous there."

"I'm fine, Tiberius!" Heiko protested, a droplet of sweat flying off him.

Tiberius studied his soldier.

"The jungle's only getting thicker, Tim," Spud said. "That clearing is our only chance to get him out."

"It also puts us off course," Tiberius said.

"I'm fine!" Heiko said adamantly.

"He's not!" Spud said equally adamantly. "And when he goes down, he's going to be a liability on the rest of us."

"We can haul him out any time," Tiberius said. "Your pilot just needs to lower a cable."

"And have the Xs scared away?"

"At least we won't be off track. Besides, they'll come back for food."

"He's a liability!"

"I know what I'm doing, Spud!"

"Do you?!"

Tiberius stepped right up to him, taller and broader. "Yes, I do. You're the one who flunked out of the uniform, remember?"

"I didn't flunk out. You shot me!"

"He shot you?" Finn asked, eyebrows popping.

Spud looked at Finn awkwardly. "You didn't hear that the other night over the Eagle-Eye?"

Finn shook his head. "We must've missed that part."

"Your brother shot you?" Grey asked, stepping forward.

Spud nodded, noticing all the eyes on them. "In the leg. Had me discharged from the military after that."

Tiberius looked at Grey, then at the other soldiers throwing them glances. "It was either me or the enemy. At least with me, I went for the leg and not the head." He looked back at Spud. "I was doing you a favor. I saved your life."

"Don't do me anymore favors," Spud said.

"Watch your step and I won't have to." He turned to Heiko. "Can you continue or not? Speak the truth."

"I'm fine, sir," Heiko replied. "It was the vine."

Tiberius gave him a firm look. "You need to stop, you tell me. Understood?"

"Sir," Heiko nodded.

Tiberius turned and signaled for them to continue forward. As he moved off, his team loyally followed.

"Oh, goody," Grey said sarcastically, walking past Spud. "We're being led by two brothers in a dick-swinging contest. This is going to end well."

Spud sighed, rubbed the back of his neck, then followed, keeping his eyes fixed on Heiko.

● ● ●

Spud moved through the now much denser vegetation with care. In particular, he veered clear of any plant that resembled the vines that had ultimately killed Foster. It was getting harder, though, as there were more and more trees. Their trunks were thinner, but with more of them it meant the gaps to walk between them were narrower. Added to this, there were a lot of fern-like plants and other types in the undergrowth that seemed to thrive in the low light. Still, there hadn't been any incidents with man-eating plants. That was good news for the time being. He just had to remember their existence on the way out again.

Heiko suddenly paused and turned to vomit.

"Let's take a break," Tiberius said, eyeing him. Heiko was sweating profusely now and looking pale and pained. "Grant, Byron, Finn, you do first watch." He moved to Heiko. "You alright?"

Heiko nodded, panting. "I just need to sit. Redress the wound." He pulled off his backpack with his good arm and slouched down on a fallen log that had made a mini clearing.

"You need to evac him now while he's still walking," Spud said.

Heiko gulped water from his canteen and Spud noticed his injured arm hung limply by his side the whole time.

"He can't even use his arm anymore."

"You need to pull him out," Grey said to Tiberius. "He's slowing us down."

Tiberius looked at her. "I make the call."

"So, make the call," she said firmly.

Tiberius looked from her to Spud.

"He didn't cut his arm on the vine, Tim," Spud said. "The venom is slowly killing him." Spud turned and walked off. He moved over to a tree trunk and leaned against it, sipped from his own canteen.

An alert sounded from Tiberius' data-band. He looked at it, then at Byron who was standing guard. "Eagle-Eye's picked something up."

Byron turned rigid and scanned the trees.

"It's a couple of klicks away," Tiberius said. "Looks

like it's headed for us. Mustn't have its camouflage on yet."

"It's coming here because it can smell Heiko's blood," Grey said.

"Finn, Lorenzo," Tiberius ordered. "Move your klauten-piss asses and go stand beside him." The two men did so, and Tiberius moved to take up Finn's perimeter position.

"We need to get him out of here," Spud said. "If it attacks, he can't defend himself."

Tiberius kept his eyes on the jungle before him. "If the ship comes now, it'll scare it off. We need to catch these fucks."

"There's no trap here, Tim," Spud said.

"If it attacks and we have to kill it, then so be it. If it's coming for us, we let it."

Spud saw something move in his peripheral vision, on the tree trunk beside him. He pushed himself away from the tree trunk, lifted his weapon and took aim.

"Damn," he panted. It was the biggest praying mantis type bug he'd ever seen. Bright yellow in color, it was the size of his forearm with chunky legs. He stared at it, not sure whether it was safe to lower his weapon. He carefully stepped away from it.

"What the fuck is that?" Jones said, raising his weapon in Heiko's direction. Finn and Lorenzo, who'd been standing either side of Heiko, but looking away from him, spun back to look at the wounded soldier. They saw a large, furry brown rodent on Heiko's arm. It was chewing at his wound.

"Shit!" Heiko stood abruptly and tried to whack it off, turning about as he flailed at it.

There were three more rodents feasting on his back.

"Fuck!" Finn said, turning his weapon on Heiko.

"What? What?" Heiko yelled.

"It's the venom!" Spud said. "He can't feel them, because his body's going numb!"

Both Finn and Lorenzo tried knocking the rodents off with the butts of their guns, but it was hard as Heiko began spinning in panicked circles. The rodents squealed and shrieked as they were battered, and within seconds more and more of them came scurrying out of a hole in the ground, climbing up all three of them.

"This is what the Xs were sent here to kill!" Grey said taking aim.

"*Rattus Carnivorous!*" Glossy's voice said over their comms.

Spud ran over and helped smack rodents off Finn with the butt of his weapon, swinging here and there between Finn and Heiko. Jones and Grey stepped forward to help both Lorenzo and Heiko too, but they were teaming over Heiko now, who was screaming in terror, and waving his good arm around trying to protect his head.

"Quiet!" Tiberius hissed.

Spud heard the rattus chewing, saw the blood sliding over Heiko's limbs and torso. Heiko dropped to his knees as they swarmed him. Grey swung her weapon like a hammer at any rattus on the ground. Jones too, as Lorenzo seemed free of them now.

"Shit!" Tiberius hissed, looking at his data-band.

"What?" Byron asked.

"It's gone. It's not showing on the Eagle-Eye's systems. The noise must've spooked it. It's in camouflage. Keep your eyes out! Forget the rats!"

"Goddamn it!" Byron hissed, raising her gun.

Grey pulled back from Heiko, swung her gun up and scanned the trees. Spud did too, leaving Finn and Lorenzo trying, but failing, to help free Heiko from the rodents covering him.

"I heard it! I heard it!" Byron said, eyes wide. "The kitten."

Spud turned toward where she was looking, just as a Panthera's growl sounded behind him. It had circled them that fast. He spun around to see the X03 lunge out of the nearby foliage onto Heiko's brown, fuzzy, rodent-filled back. Lorenzo and Finn stumbled back, flipped their guns over and fired at it, as did Grey, but they weren't fast enough. The X swiftly hauled Heiko's body into the leaves, as the remaining rodents scattered. Some ran up the legs of Finn and Lorenzo, and somehow one ended up on Spud's arm. He felt its teeth sink into his flesh.

"Ah, fuck!" he winced, punching it off. It fell to the ground, and he shot it.

Byron yelled from the other side of their group, as more rodents charged out of the scrub in her direction.

"It must be the blood!" Grant yelled. "They can smell the blood!"

"Kill them!" Tiberius yelled, firing at the rodents, along with Grant, Jones and Byron.

"Heiko!" Lorenzo, now rodent free, yelled toward the plants through which Heiko had disappeared.

"Come on!" Grey said, charging after the Panthera.

"Shit!" Spud said, running after her. Finn and Lorenzo followed, leaving Tiberius, Grant, Jones and Byron dealing with the rodents.

They plunged through the plant life, following the trail of blood in a haunting replay of what happened with Foster. They could hear the X ahead of them. The one good thing about the X carrying Heiko's body, was that it was weighed down and not as fast as it would normally be.

He heard the other group firing and screaming and wondered what was happening.

"We gotta go back," Spud said to the others. "We're safer together."

"We're close," Grey puffed, jogging along, jumping over rocks and logs and shrubs.

She came to a halt as they saw Heiko laying there face down. Spud didn't even notice the wounds from the rattus. All he saw was what the X had done to him. Heiko's back was torn open so badly that his spine was poking through and had snapped in two.

Something large and heavy suddenly thudded into Spud from behind.

He slammed into the ground, winded, as gunfire and sparks of light overwhelmed his senses. Pain shot through him. And just as fast as it started, it ended. He saw a large furless claw fall down by his face. In fact, it was the size of his face, and the claws were dripping with blood.

The weight suddenly lifted and someone hauled him to his feet. Tiberius stared at him. More gunfire sounded as Grey ensured the creature was dead.

"You alright?" His brother's worried eyes stared into his.

"What the fuck happened?" Spud said, looking around at the dead Panthera on the ground.

"Grant was handling all the rattus, so I came to—"

"Save my ass," Spud finished for him, staring at the dead Panthera.

"Don't sound so grateful."

"Fuck," Lorenzo said, eyes lowered as he knelt by Heiko's body.

Tiberius stared at him, saw Heiko's lifeless eyes. His face fell, briefly, worry and maybe guilt flashing across it, then his expression hardened again.

"Get up," he said to Lorenzo. "Let's move. There're still three out there."

Grant, Byron and Jones joined them, their eyes not resting long on Heiko's mutilated body, before they fixed on the jungle around them.

"The Eagle-Eye will leave a marker for him," Tiberius said. "We'll get him on the way back."

Spud grimaced and reached around to touch his back. He pulled his hand away and saw blood on his fingers.

"Your back's cut up," Finn said, pulling medical supplies out of his backpack. "Sit down."

"Always the back," Spud groaned.

"Lucky you had the anti-venom," Grey said, a crack showing in her controlled facade.

"Shirt," Finn said. Spud pulled his shirt up and Finn very swiftly and efficiently dressed the cuts from the X's claws.

"You're getting quite the collection of X scars," Grey said, eyeing his back. She held out her canteen of water. He took it and gave a pained smile.

"Yeah, but chicks dig scarred guys, right?"

Her face gave nothing away. "Shut up and drink."

CHAPTER NINE

They said their goodbyes to Heiko and continued forward solemnly, and maybe even a little rattled. Tiberius' unit didn't seem so nonchalant now and he noticed them paying more mind to Spud's crew. One death they could put down to bad luck, but two? They finally realized these creatures were expert killers.

Spud bandaged the rattus bite mark on his arm, noticing that both Finn and Lorenzo had them too. He guessed the rodents weren't deterred by klauten piss like the Pantheras were. That said, the klauten piss hadn't totally deterred the Panthera. Spud eyed Finn and Lorenzo and saw the thick yellow paste covering them was starting to wear off in the humidity. The Panthera hadn't attacked them, but it hadn't hesitated to attack those near them.

"Tiberius?" Nikita's voice sounded over their comms.

"Yeah?" he answered.

"The *Gabriel*'s Science Officer, Dr. Carlton, wants to know why there are two dead X03s."

Tiberius stopped walking. "What?"

"He wants the last three to be captured alive."

"They're watching our comms," Spud told him.

"Yeah?" Tiberius said to Nikita. "Did they see two of my men get killed?"

"They don't care, Tim," Spud said. "Look at me. I'm facing jail, not because I gave my thieving ex a ride, but because I helped kill their expensive X." He exchanged a look with Grey. "Her, too," he told Tiberius. "She didn't steal anything. But she helped me kill their expensive weapon. They want us to pay for that."

"We're here because we know too much," Finn added. "It may not be the admiral, per se. It's probably the folks on Quadrant Four insisting on this."

"That's where these things came from?" Tiberius asked.

Finn nodded. "They have a lot of power. More than you think."

Tiberius looked at Spud with concern.

"You knew about Quadrant Four?" Spud asked, eyes narrowed with accusation.

"Just rumors," Tiberius said. "Nothing confirmed until now."

Nikita's voice sounded again. "Capture the last three alive and there'll be no penalty."

The silence sat thickly in the jungle's humidity.

"They told me to say that," Nikita added. "In case you hadn't figured it out."

Tiberius turned and stared quietly out into the distance. His mind was turning over, perhaps finally realizing just what he'd stepped into. Spud felt a lump of guilt stick in his throat. Fight as they may, Tim was still his brother.

"I'm sorry Dad sent you here," he told him.

Tiberius looked back at him. "He didn't send me. I volunteered."

"You volunteered for this?" Spud's brow furrowed.

Tiberius nodded. "I was there when he got the call about you. He asked me to step outside the room. Next thing I know, he calls me in and says you got yourself in trouble and have to do a mission for the navy to dig your way out. He wouldn't tell me what the mission was, but I sensed it was dangerous. So, I volunteered to watch your back and make sure you weren't going to get yourself killed." He gave a laugh. "No wonder Dad tried to stop me from coming."

"So he offers me up on a plate, but tries to protect you?"

Tiberius turned his back on Spud and raised his data-band, pulling up the map showing the location of the X03 traps.

Grey eyed Spud sympathetically. He turned and walked away, trying to gather his thoughts and breath, as the others stole glances between him and Tiberius.

The sound of a kitten's cry stopped him in his tracks, however.

He stiffened and jumped back, raising his gun. He saw the undergrowth before him move, but it confused him. The movement was too small to be an X.

But he heard it again. The soft kitten's cry.

He slid backwards, gun fixed on the undergrowth.

Then he saw it.

It was an *actual* kitten.

Well, a small cat. Not a newborn, more like a toddler. A furry, tabby thing with tufts of hair atop its pointy ears and a tail that didn't quite reach mid-shin.

It cried again and peered out at him, blue eyes imploring. He lowered his weapon and watched, stunned, as the kitten cautiously came out and curiously sniffed the barrel of his gun, then his boot, then brushed itself against his leg.

"What the hell?" Grey said, lining it up in her weapon's sight.

Spud raised his hand to stop her, as the others watched. Spud eyed it carefully, then slowly crouched and held out his hand to it.

"Spud," Finn said, "are you sure about that?"

"Not really," he said, extending his fingers toward it. The kitten looked up and brushed its face against his fingers, purring loudly as it did. Suddenly its tabby fur blinked in and out of a mirage-like state. Spud pulled his fingers back.

"It's one of them..." he said.

"It can't be," he heard Glossy's voice say over their comms. "They made them sterile. There's a bare minimum of information on the mission files, but that's in there. The X03s are all female and they're sterile."

"Yeah, well, I'm looking at a baby X right in front of me."

"Do they lose their fur as they get older?" Finn asked, studying it, confused.

The kitten brushed past Spud's leg again and gave

another cry. Spud moved backward from it.

"How can it breed?" Byron asked.

"The fur…" Finn said, thinking aloud. "Maybe it bred with a native wildcat or lynx or something."

"But it's supposed to be sterile!" Jones said.

The kitten jumped up, raising its front legs on Spud. He stumbled back in fright, falling on his back. He winced, reminded of his fresh cuts.

"Shit!" He raised his gun as the kitten climbed up his leg and made its way toward his face. He aimed the muzzle as best he could at the kitten's face. It cried again and rubbed its neck against the muzzle, scratching it.

"Jesus," Lorenzo said. "It's like a real kitty."

Spud, panting, looked into the kitten's blue eyes. He pushed it off and stood up.

"Should we kill it?" Grant asked.

"If it's gonna grow to be one of them…" Lorenzo raised his gun, but Spud knocked the weapon down.

"It's not a threat."

"Yeah, but in a few months' time?"

Spud looked back at the kitten. "It's not an X. It's only half of one."

"Half is enough," Lorenzo moved to fire, but Spud stopped him again.

"Maybe it inherited good genes from its other parent."

"Speaking of parents, where is its mother?" Grey asked.

"Here," Tiberius said.

They turned to see Tiberius looking past a clump of fern-like plants. They peered over and saw some kind of large native cat with the same tufts of hair atop its pointy ears, its gut torn open and innards spilt, with dead, half-eaten baby kittens around it.

"The X ate it," Finn said. "Even the young... It saw them as a threat."

"It sees everything as a threat," Spud said.

"What the hell is this?" Byron said, hooking something on the barrel of her weapon and lifting it out of the grass. It was shreds of skin and fur. Spud remembered the skin in the box on the *Benobi.*

"They grow fast," he said. "They shed their skin as they do."

"Ew," Byron said, throwing the skin off.

"It must belong to this cat," Finn said, looking at the surviving larger kitten as it cried and rubbed itself along Spud's leg again.

"The kill looks several hours old," Grant said, eyeing the carcass. "The kitten must be hungry."

Tiberius looked at it. "That's not our problem." He checked his data-band. "We need to get to the traps and try and catch the last three. The nearest trap is 15 klicks due east. The Eagle-Eye is telling us the path is clear."

Skeptical faces stared back at him.

"You're really going to try and take them alive?" Spud asked.

Tiberius nodded. "What choice do we have? Admiral's orders."

Spud felt a sharp pain in his leg and looked down to see the kitten climbing him. Its blue eyes stared up as it cried again. He reached down and pulled it off him. "Leave me alone."

"It'll be dark soon," Grey said. "Time's wasting."

"Let's move out!" Tiberius said, then set off.

Spud moved after the team. When he looked back, he saw the kitten trotting after him.

"No," he told it. He walked on some more, then looked back to see it still following.

He sighed, then opened his pack and pulled out a ration bar. He took a bite, then tore a small chunk off and threw it into the jungle. The kitten chased after it, disappearing into the shrubs.

Spud turned and continued on.

CHAPTER TEN

Another few hours had passed with no sightings of the three remaining Pantheras. The sky was beginning to darken.

"Can they climb?" Tiberius asked Spud.

"The X03s?" Spud recalled it running at him on the *Benobi* and scaling the walls as it did. He nodded. "Yeah. They can climb. They have claws like steel."

"Where the hell are we going to sleep?" Jones asked.

"On the ground," Tiberius said. "With our eyes open." He exchanged a look with Spud. "We'll set up laser trip-sensors around us, 100 meters out."

Suddenly the ground rumbled beneath their feet. Everyone paused and looked down at it.

"Grindow," Grant said, pointing to the volcano's peak

visible in the near distance through a gap in the trees.

"Is it going to blow?" Byron asked. "That felt like it was going to blow."

"Nikita?" Spud asked.

"Wait a moment," Nikita replied over their comms. "Science officer says it's just the plates shifting. There's no immediate threat."

"Yeah, right," Spud said. "This is why we couldn't wait for Tiberius' crew to get the anti-venom. Because they were scared it was going to blow."

They stared at Grindow's Peak as though waiting to see if smoke or lava was going to start spewing forth. It didn't.

"Tiberius," Grant said rubbing his scarred cheek.

"Yeah."

"Of all the missions we've done together, this isn't my favorite."

"Yeah," Tiberius nodded, eyes fixed on the volcano. "Mine either."

● ● ●

After establishing a laser trip-sensor perimeter, each device covering 20 meters wide and 10 meters high, they set up camp for the night inside a cluster of narrow tree trunks that formed a rough oval shape, essentially providing them with a wooden cell. While four bodies huddled close together inside trying to get some sleep, the other four stood guard around them, ensuring one of the klauten-piss boys was always on duty.

The air was warm and the motorcycle mosquitos drove them crazy, hooning past their ears loudly. The jungle floor was dark, no stars or sky to be seen above.

Spud took first watch with Tiberius, Byron and Lorenzo. They stood in silence, constantly checking their data-bands for input from the Eagle-Eye. But the truth was the jungle was so thick here, he wasn't sure they could trust the Eagle-Eye for protection. If they ever could before.

"Cover me," Tiberius said, lowering his gun and slinging it over his shoulder.

"Where you going?" Spud asked.

"To take a leak. That alright?"

Spud watched him walk away. "I'll come."

Tiberius shot him a look but didn't argue it. "Lorenzo, Byron, stay sharp."

They gave a firm nod, eyes scanning carefully, hyperalert.

Tiberius didn't move very far out. Spud stood close by him, searching the darkness.

"So," Spud whispered, "about what you said before..."

Tiberius, in midstream, glanced over his shoulder at Spud. "What about it?"

"You really volunteered for this?"

"You don't believe me?"

"I know Dad and I weren't exactly best buddies, but I'm struggling to comprehend that he's okay with me dying here."

"He not okay with you dying, Spud. And he didn't want you rotting in a jail either."

Spud shrugged. "If I made it out alive, I'm a hero. If I die, I'm a hero. Either way he can celebrate me and use it for leverage with the public."

Tiberius looked at him as he zipped. "Jesus, Spud. That's cold. He's not like that and you know it."

Spud stared back. "Don't tell me the Senator couldn't have pulled some strings to get me out of this."

"Like you'd be happy with him interfering in your life. You made it clear you wanted him to stay away when you left the navy, Spel."

"What I don't get, is why he let you come?" Spud said. "Or was the Senator so blind and naive that he didn't really know what he was sending you to, here on Bracken-Loti?"

"He *didn't* know, Spel. He was told it was a dangerous mission, but what mission isn't? He wasn't happy about me coming here and I think it's because he didn't have all the details."

"Because you were his favorite," Spud nodded.

"And why do you think that is, Spel?" Tiberius said impatiently.

Spud shrugged. "Because I didn't want to fight wars we had no business fighting?"

"You think that's it?" Tiberius asked. "You really don't get it, do you?"

"Get what?"

"You pulled away from the family as soon as you could. If you'd been paying attention, you would've figured it out by now."

"Figured what out?"

Tiberius ignored him, checking his data-band.

"Figured what out?" Spud asked again.

"Now's not the time, Spel. We'll talk about it after."

"And if we don't make it off this rock?"

Tiberius looked away.

"What?" Spud demanded, albeit his voice was still a whisper so as not to wake the others. "You're hiding something."

"I'm not hiding anything, Spel. It's always been there staring me in the face. I can't believe you haven't worked it out yet."

"Worked what out?" Spud hissed, starting to get shitty.

Tiberius ignored him.

"Worked what out?" Spud hissed again more firmly, stepping closer.

"That you're not his!" Tiberius snapped, before regret washed over his face.

"Not his what?" Spud's face suddenly went from all screwed-up to flat as a pancake, as the truth dawned on him. "I'm not *his*? Not Dad's?"

Tiberius eyed him in the glow of his data-band.

"I'm not his kid?" Spud asked, his voice lacking volume. "Then whose am I?"

"I don't know," Tiberius said softly. "I just know you're not his."

Spud felt weakened, the cuts on his back suddenly stinging with impunity. He looked back at Tiberius. "Mom?"

"Relax. You're hers. I was there when you were born."

"But...?"

"What's the one thing you know about Dad?" Tiberius asked. "He's all about appearances." Tiberius gave a laugh, checking the data-band again. "It's my first memory, you know? Mom and Dad arguing about her affair."

"Mom cheated on him?" Spud gaped.

"To be fair, he cheated on her first. I remember that from the argument too. But I guess she got him back, huh? She had her lover's child and made him raise you."

Spud looked away, winded. "*Fuck*... No wonder he never liked me."

"It's not that he didn't like you, Spud. He still raised you as his own, didn't he? He just... didn't like what you reminded him of. The guy Mom fell in love with."

Spud looked back at Tiberius. "She loved him?"

Tiberius nodded. "That's what they were arguing about. Dad had him sent away to a far-off planet, so he could never see either of you again."

"Who was he?" Spud asked quietly.

"I don't know."

"Why didn't you tell me this until now?" Spud asked, unable to hide the hurt from his voice.

Tiberius shrugged. "I was hoping you would figure it out yourself."

"Jesus... We're stuck on a planet with a bunch of X03s trying to kill us, and now you dump *this* shit on me?"

"Hey, you asked me to tell you."

"Why *did* you tell me? And why did you volunteer to come here?"

"I told you! To save your ass!" he hissed. "Trust me, he begged me, *threatened* me, not to do it."

"But you did. Why?"

"Because Dad's forgotten what it's like to be a soldier!" He stepped right up to Spud, hissing quietly. "It's been a long time since he wore a uniform. He's spent too long in the halls of politics now, where one's objectives outweigh the lives of the people around you." He poked a finger into Spud's chest. "I still wear this uniform, Spud, and when you wear the uniform you live by a code and that code is to *never* leave anyone alive in the field. We gotta have each other's back. We might not share the same birth father, Spel, but we do share our mother." He stabbed him in the chest again. "You are my brother, whether he likes it or not, and I will not leave you here to die!"

Spud stepped backward. "Fuck, man..."

Tiberius clenched his jaw. "My soldiers are my brothers. *You* are my brother. And I always have my brothers' back. I will *not* let you die."

Spud's eyes stung with emotion as he stared back at his brother, the great Tiberius. "You really are the hero they make you out to be, aren't you?"

"I'm not a hero, Spud. I'm just a guy trying to do his job, while this myth grows every day and overshadows me. Do you know what it's like to have to live up to this fucking legend every day? Everyone watching the every move of the great Tiberius? I have my faults, trust me. As do *you*, little brother."

Spud looked to the ground, a little ashamed. Tiberius sighed.

"If I pushed you," he said, "it was because I wanted you to impress the old man. If you lived up to his expectations, then maybe he'd treat you like he did me."

Silence sat for a moment.

"God," Spud nodded to himself, "I was an asshole, wasn't I?"

"You were a brat sometimes, yeah," Tiberius nodded, "but I guess I was, too."

"What the hell are you two doing," Byron called out in an angry whisper, moving closer, "jerking each other off?!"

Spud looked back at her. "*Ew*. We're brothers."

Tiberius smiled, and slapped Spud on the back.

"Ow," Spud flinched.

"Oops. Sorry." Tiberius moved toward Byron.

"Tim?" Spud said.

Tiberius turned around.

"I won't let you die, either," Spud said.

Tiberius stared at him a moment, then gave him a nod, and took up his position again.

CHAPTER ELEVEN

The night passed without incident, and Spud managed, mainly through exhaustion, to get a few hours' sleep. He awoke, however, to something tickling his face.

At the sound of a kitten's cry he sat up, terrified. A lump of fluffy fur fell into his lap and blue eyes looked up at him.

"Shit!" he panted.

"Looks like you have an admirer," Grey said, looking down at him as the kitten raised its front legs onto his chest and stretched.

Spud rubbed his eyes and felt it climb up his chest to his face and brush its jaw against his. He grabbed it and pulled it back, his shirt caught in its claws.

"What the hell does it want from me?" he asked.

"It likes you," Grey smirked, as Jones narrowed his eyes at them, shaking his head.

"Trust me to attract a woman who could kill me," Spud said, shooting Grey a look. She suppressed a smile as she turned away.

Spud stood and lowered the kitten to the ground. "*Shoo!*"

It ignored him, brushing against his leg. He sighed.

"Did you feed it?" Lorenzo asked.

Spud looked at him guiltily.

"Big mistake," Lorenzo said. "It thinks you're its mommy now."

"Oh, no—"

"If it's alright with you," Tiberius said, "we have three Pantheras to catch."

Spud nodded and grabbed his squad weapon.

"What are we going to use for bait?" Grant said, stepping forward.

"You mean aside from us?" Byron said dryly.

The kitten meowed, and they all looked down at it.

● ● ●

They came upon the first trap after a couple of hours. It was a large, rectangular metal cage, painted a jungle green, in a tight clearing. The controls sat in a box strapped to the inside, which they swiftly removed. A test showed that once the door closed, shutters were released and the cage became a completely sealed box — similar to the one the X arrived in on the *Benobi*. There was, however, a small panel in the top side of the box, which they assumed was either for lowering food inside, or perhaps an exit for whatever bait lured the X inside.

"Don't look at me like that," Spud said as the kitten's blue eyes stared up at him. He was backing into the trap and trying to lure the kitten after him. "We've got a nice spot for you to sleep. Here," he pulled some of his ration bar off and waved it at the kitten. It sniffed the air. "Come on, girl. Wait. Are you even a girl?" He tilted his head trying to look under it.

"It's a girl," Lorenzo said while carefully checking the data from the Eagle-Eye. "I got cats at home."

"Come on, girl," Spud said.

"Wouldn't one of us be more appetizing?" Jones asked.

"Of course," Grant said, "but wouldn't you rather it ate this kitten?"

"Don't listen to them, Baby-X," Spud said to it. "We're not going to let anything happen to you." He waggled the portion of ration bar and it crept up to him and ate it. He reached out and gave it a pat. "I think she's smart. She knows we're up to something."

"Alright," Tiberius said. "Klauten-piss boys, you each get into a tree and make sure you stay downwind." Lorenzo and Finn gave a nod, picked a tree and began to climb. "Everyone else take position on the ground and keep your eyes sharp. Stay in twos, back-to-back. Be ready."

They nodded and spread out. Spud was paired with Byron, Grey with Jones, Finn with Grant, while Tiberius climbed a third tree and managed the controls for the trap. The only trouble was, Baby-X didn't want to stay put and kept following Spud as he tried to leave the trap.

"Shit, you're like a dog," he muttered and picked up the blue-eyed furball. "Tiberius?"

"Yeah?"

"Take my spot with Byron. Looks like I gotta be the live bait."

"Spud?" Finn asked, concerned.

"She's not going to stay here without me. I guess two targets for the X is better than none."

"We've got your back, brother," Tiberius said as he moved to take up Spud's position.

"I'm holding you to that."

The two locked eyes before Spud moved back inside the cage with the Baby-X. He sat down beneath the opening in the roof, gun fixed on the mouth of the trap, while the Baby-X curled up in his lap for sleep.

Hours passed and nothing.

Spud was struggling to keep his eyes open. He could feel the Baby-X's sleeping purrs reverberating through his legs and it was rather soothing.

"Spud!" Tiberius barked.

He opened his eyes.

"Stay alert, goddamn it."

"Well, if you could hurry that X along, that'd be great."

"Careful what you wish for," Grey said.

The ground suddenly shook. More violently than last time. Spud grabbed the side of the cage to hold on as the Baby-X awoke and dug her claws into his thighs.

"*Aargh.*" He pulled the Baby-X off his lap. "Could you *not* do that?"

After a moment's stillness, the ground shook again and a loud boom sounded. The shaking was so violent, Spud thought the trap was going to roll over. He heard a yell and thump. As soon as the shaking stopped, he pulled himself up to see through the metal bars that

Lorenzo had fallen down from his tree.

"Fuck!" Lorenzo moaned, holding his arm.

Spud saw Tiberius race over to help him up. Lorenzo held his shoulder wincing. Spud could tell from where he was that Lorenzo's shoulder wasn't sitting right.

"It's dislocated," Tiberius looked to the others. "Jones! A hand!"

Jones quickly joined the two men and Spud watched nervously as they worked to put Lorenzo's shoulder back in place.

The Baby-X meowed low. Spud looked down to see its ears pinned back. It shivered and shook and its mirage state engaged on and off.

"It's just the volcano," Spud tried to placate it. "It's the least of our problems right now."

"Oh, Spud," Nikita's voice sounded over their comms. "I'm not so sure about that. Take a look."

"Uh oh..." Grey said. Spud followed her eyes but couldn't see what she was looking at. He removed his backpack and moved further along the cage until he saw the top of Grindow's Peak in the near distance.

It was smoking.

"Oh shit," Spud said. "Nik, how long until that thing blows?"

"I'm on it," Nikita said, before silence fell over the line.

Suddenly the Eagle-Eye began chirping an alarm. Tiberius dropped Lorenzo's arm and looked at his data-band.

"Fuck! *Fuck*!" he said getting to his feet. "There're two on approach! I repeat two Pantheras on approach." He swung his gun over his shoulder, grabbing Lorenzo and pulling him to his feet. "One from north-west and one due north! Get into position!"

"Shit!" Spud said, darting his eyes between the jungle and the smoking Grindow. Baby-X meowed again from beside Spud. It was low and terrifying, making the hairs on Spud's arms stand on end. Baby-X's ears were still pinned back, its back hunching, its eyes fixed on the mouth of the shrubs. Spud raised his gun. "Maybe you should get behind me, Baby-X."

The kitten didn't move. It stuck close to Spud's side.

"We've lost contact!" Tiberius yelled. "They've engaged camouflage!"

A loud screech suddenly pierced their ears. Spud saw a family of those brightly colored parrot-type birds fly speedily overhead. Their target, the Eagle-Eye.

The large birds swooped on the Eagle-Eye from all sides, attacking it with fury. Pecking it, clawing it and breaking it apart.

"Fuck!" Tiberius yelled, as the destroyed Eagle-Eye dropped to the ground in pieces. The birds then suddenly turned and swooped for Finn, perched up a nearby tree. Finn began swatting them in self-defense, as they pecked and clawed him. On the other side of the tree, hidden behind some large leaves, Spud spied a nest.

"Oh, shit! Finn! Get out of the tree! It's their nest!"

Finn's eyes popped and he swiftly dropped to the ground and rolled, his arms bloodied from their black beaks. The birds swooped down after him.

"Run!" Spud yelled at him.

Movement in the shrubs caught Spud's eye. The ground shook again and he fell backward in the trap.

Baby-X hissed viciously. Spud clung to the side of the cage, watching as the large parrots tried to pick Finn up and fly away. Spud raised his weapon around the side of the cage and fired near them to scare them away. The birds dropped Finn and he hit the ground with a thud. The shrubs shook again on one side, then on the other.

"Incoming!" Grant yelled.

"Both sides!" Tiberius yelled.

Byron and Jones started firing. Spud paused, not sure what he was seeing. A miraged-X lunged out of the shrubs with speed and seemed to whiz around the tree trunk the soldiers stood next to. Byron stepped back, but Jones moved too late and the X slammed into him.

Gunfire rained upward from Jones' gun but he wasn't really firing it. Spud saw the young corporal was almost decapitated from one crunch of the X's jaws.

Byron screamed and fired at the creature. Spud saw the second camouflaged X charging her from behind. He ran out of the trap, firing at it. It skidded and fled back into the shrubs.

More gunfire sounded on the other side. Grant and Tiberius were firing at something.

"It's all three!" Tiberius yelled.

"They're hunting in a pack!" Grey yelled, firing at one of the others.

The X that Spud had fired at, charged out of the undergrowth going for Byron again. It knocked her down, camouflaged jaw clamping on her gun, ripping it from her hands. Spud charged at it, ramming himself into it before the creature could tear into her. The X swiped at him, caught his shoulder. Spud yelled in pain. Byron recovered, swiftly grabbed her weapon and fired at it, catching it in the leg. It whined and charged her again. Spud slammed the butt of his weapon into its back. The X flung him backward like a rag doll and lunged for Byron again. She screamed and threw her gun up again in defense. The X's jaws hit it with a sound like metal on metal. Spud recovered, grabbed his gun, saw a clear enough shot and fired. The bullet grazed its neck and with a whine, it let Byron's gun go and raced back into the undergrowth.

An agonizing scream sounded on the other side of the trap and Spud looked around to see Grant fall forward with a miraged X on his back. His backpack had been torn off, and the creature's jaws fixed to his flesh as it began shaking him like a toy. Tiberius fired and hit it, but the X bounced up and scooted away, moving so fast their heads were spinning. The ground shook violently again and they all lost their footing. The X saw its chance and quickly reappeared. Tiberius barely had time to roll over on his back before the miraged X was on him, snapping at his arm, his leg, trying to drag him away. Tim yelled in pain.

"NO!" Spud shouted, running for him. Tiberius was using his weapon for protection, hitting it with the butt of his gun, but Spud saw the blood running down his arm and leg. Spud fired, hit the X and it ran away hissing. Spud ran for Tim, saw his arm and leg were shredded with deep cuts. He pulled him to sit up, before his brother yelled, "Watch out!"

Spud spun around to see the X charging them again. Gunfire rang out and Spud looked to see Grey aiming. She hit her target with a barrage of bullets, splashing blood across its miraged state, felling it. Byron joined her to ensure it was dead.

"Grey! Behind!" Finn yelled, raising his weapon and firing.

Spud's eyes widened as he saw one of the other

camouflaged X03s lunging behind her. Finn missed as the camouflaged body slammed into her, knocking her down and tearing her backpack away. Spud got to his feet and ran for her as the X clamped its jaws into her back. She screamed and Spud tried to fire, but he was out of ammo. Still sprinting toward them, he raised the gun and slammed it into the X's head. It let her go, stepped backward, shook its head as though to clear it, and growled at Spud, but as it went to lunge at him, its head suddenly exploded in a hail of bullets and a cloud of blood and brains. Spud raised his hand to shield his eyes from its splattering bodily fluids. When he looked again, he saw Finn jogging toward them and lowering his gun.

Spud dropped to his knees beside Grey. Her back was torn open real bad. He pulled off his overshirt and pressed it against her wounds.

"It's gonna be okay!" he told her. "We're going to get you out of here."

She groaned in agony.

"There's still one out there somewhere!" Byron yelled, reloading.

Spud glanced at Finn. "Get my brother."

Finn jogged to Tiberius, and Byron joined him, weapon ready. Spud looked around to see who was left alive.

"Grant?" Spud asked, although he knew the answer. Lorenzo shook his head, as Byron and Finn dragged Tiberius over.

"Spud," Nikita's voice sounded. "You got anything from a few hours to a few days before Grindow blows. But by the look of that thing, I'd say a few hours."

"We're not going to make it back to the Hacienda,"

Finn said, wincing at his own cuts, made by the angry parrots, as he and Lorenzo stood either side, weapons raised to the jungle, although Spud noted that Lorenzo was holding his gun in his left hand and the guy was clearly right-handed.

"The last X is injured," Spud said. "It took a bullet to the leg and neck, I think. It's injured."

"But it's still alive," Finn said. "It's out there and it's pissed, and our numbers are down."

Tiberius, Grey and Lorenzo were wounded and of little help to the team. Byron, Finn and Spud were the only ones still useful.

"The navy's gonna be pissed we killed their Pantheras," Byron said.

"They can bill me," Tiberius breathed through his pain.

"Spud!" Nikita said over their comms. "We're coming to get you. We'll cable you out."

"No," Tiberius groaned, "if Grindow blows the ship's fucked."

Spud glanced at the smoking Grindow nearby, its rim burning and bubbling with bright orange lava. "We can't risk it," he panted.

"We're not leaving you, Spud!" Glossy said.

"I'm not asking you to," he said. "Just let me think."

"Spud," Nikita said, "if you can get to that clearing we were going to pick up Heiko from, I can get you out of there. It should be a safe enough distance away from Grindow."

"How far?" Spud asked.

"Five klicks due east from where you are."

Spud winced, anguished.

"We can't carry them and defend ourselves," Finn

said, reading Spud's thoughts as he looked at Tiberius and Grey.

"I can walk," Tiberius groaned as Byron finished tying a tourniquet around his thigh.

"But can you run? Can you shoot?" Spud asked looking at his torn-up arm.

"Haven't you heard?" Tiberius managed a pained smile. "I'm the great Tiberius."

"You can't carry me. I'll slow you down," Grey said, looking away. "Go."

Spud grabbed her chin and turned her face back toward him. "You're making it out alive, Grey. You wouldn't want to disappoint me, would you?"

She managed a brief smile before she groaned in pain again.

"You saved me on the *Benobi*," he told her. "I'm saving you on Bracken-Loti."

The ground rumbled violently and the Baby-X came out of the trap, running over to Spud's side. He stared at it, then at the trap, his mind ticking over.

A realization hit him.

"She's our warning system," he breathed.

"What?" Lorenzo said, using his good arm to support his injured shoulder.

"Baby-X," he said. "She sensed the Pantheras before we did. Forget the Eagle-Eye, she's our warning system! She'll know when it's close." He looked at Finn. "We make a stretcher, put Grey on it." He turned to Lorenzo. "Are your legs good?"

He nodded.

"If we strap her to you, can you pull her stretcher along?"

Lorenzo nodded again. "Yeah."

"Byron," Spud said, "you help Tiberius walk. Finn and I," he picked up the kitten, "and Baby-X, will guard you. We stay together, in a tight group. We can make it."

They all stared back at him with hope, nodding.

Tiberius smiled and held his hand out. Spud clasped his hand around it.

"You'd make a good soldier, you know that?" Tiberius said.

Spud smiled back. "Yeah, I know. I just didn't want it." Spud pulled his brother to his feet. "Let's get this stretcher done, now!"

CHAPTER TWELVE

They locked the bodies of Grant and Jones in the trap where they would be safe from further predators, then set off at a steady pace for the clearing with the dead soldiers' weapons and ammo. They didn't get far, though, before the ground rumbled and another sonic boom sounded. Lorenzo lost his feet, the stretcher hit the ground and Grey groaned. Spud quickly moved to help Lorenzo right himself.

"You good?"

Lorenzo nodded and straightened the strap around his neck and good shoulder, which was tied to the stretcher behind. Spud gave him a nod and moved to Grey, gently clasping her shoulder. "You're doing good,

Grey. Hang in there!"

"Shit! Spud..." Finn said, pointing up at Grindow's Peak. Spud saw flecks of bright orange lava shooting

"Shit! Spud..." Finn said, pointing up at Grindow's Peak. Spud saw flecks of bright orange lava shooting upwards. The bubbling lava was now fully boiling.

"Move, move, move!" Spud yelled, charging ahead. "That thing is going to blow soon!"

Finn led the charge, weapon swinging back and forth, while Byron and Tiberius limped behind him. Next, Lorenzo pulled Grey's sled, while Spud covered their rear with the Baby-X strapped in a small makeshift sack made from his cut up backpack at his chest. As he moved backward, sweeping his weapon across the jungle, he stole looks at the cat to check her demeanor for any sign the last X was on their tail.

Tired, hungry, muscles aching, wounds stinging, sweat dripping, they continued the charge toward their rendezvous. Spud stole glances at their two klauten-piss men, Finn and Lorenzo, and noticed the thick paste had worn off even more since he'd last checked. Still, they had some, and they were with them.

"You're three klicks out from the clearing," Glossy reported anxiously over their comms.

Spud nodded. "Roger that."

Lorenzo paused, panting from the exhaustion of pulling Grey's sled, when the Baby-X dug its claws into Spud's chest. He flinched and darted a glance to it. The kitten's ears were pinned back.

"It's close!" Spud called. Lorenzo straightened and looked around.

"Keep moving! Keep moving!" Finn said.

They stepped up their pace, darting nervous glances

at the jungle around them. Spud turned the Baby-X around in her sack and swung her around like his weapon, trying to get a lock on the X's direction. Dead ahead, the Baby-X stared into the leaves and hissed.

"She's right behind us!" Spud saw movement and fired. The Baby-X ducked its head inside the sack at the noise, digging its claws into his skin again.

"Spud? Talk to me!" Finn called, checking on him.

"Keep moving!" he called back.

More movement, Spud fired again. Byron and Tiberius stopped, turned around and raised their weapons.

"I said keep moving!" Spud yelled.

"There's only one," Tiberius yelled back, "the more guns we put on it the greater our chances."

"I'll hold it off!" Spud yelled, firing again. "You keep moving. Get Grey out of here!"

"More macho bullshit!" they heard a craggy voice yell.

Spud risked a glance to see Dr. McLaren roll in on a small, silent, electric four-wheeler buggy with an attached small trailer.

"Holy shit!" Byron called.

Baby-X hissed again and Spud turned back to shoot again.

"Grindow is about to blow, you idiots!" McLaren grumbled. "You need to get out of here!"

"We're trying!" Spud yelled.

McLaren pulled up alongside Grey's sled. "Put her on the back."

Finn and Byron moved to free Grey from the sled.

"Get her to the clearing!" Spud ordered McLaren, noticing he didn't have space for them all. "Lorenzo,

Tiberius, go with her!"

"I'm staying with you, brother!" Tiberius said.

"No, Tim! You're fucking injured. You'll get yourself killed! Go with her!"

Baby-X hissed again, and Spud turned and fired. He saw the X that time. It was getting closer. "Go!" he yelled over his shoulder. "That's an order! Get out of here!"

Tiberius fired into the jungle, ignoring him.

Spud moved up to his brother, snatched the pistol from Tim's belt and shot him in the leg.

"Fuck!" Tiberius yelled as he dropped to the ground.

"I'm saving your life," Spud said. "Get out of here! *Go!*"

Grey was now on the buggy's back tray and Lorenzo was holding her best he could with his good arm. McLaren revved the quiet engine ready to go. Finn fell back and hauled Tiberius into the buggy beside McLaren, while Spud and Byron fired into the leaves.

"Get on, you useless lump of meat!" McLaren barked at Tiberius. As soon as he did, McLaren swerved around and took off.

"We'll be waiting for you, Spud!" Nikita's voice sounded over the comms. "You just got two and a half klicks to go!"

Spud, Finn and Byron breathed heavily, sweeping their weapons across the jungle. Though he was nervous at having less guns on the X, he was glad he no longer had to worry about the wounded. They could move faster now.

"We just need to hold it off," Spud panted. "We lead it to the clearing, and Nik will shred it with the dropship's guns."

"I'm looking forward to it," Finn said, as Byron nodded, her eyes wide with adrenaline.

Baby-X suddenly climbed out of her sling and hung over Spud's shoulder, claws digging into his skin. He spun around as she hissed, and fired. The X growled back. Loudly. Angrily.

"Oh... she's pissed," Byron said.

"Yeah, she is," Spud said. "She can't sneak up on us now we have a secret weapon."

"Smartest thing you ever did was feed that kitten," Finn said.

"Oh, yeah," Spud nodded.

More movement, Finn fired. A flock of parrots screeched as they zoomed overhead. The ground rumbled again, long and deep.

Very long and *very* deep.

Spud glanced around. "Thaaaaat did not feel good."

"No," Finn agreed.

"Let's step it up," Spud said. "Backs together, eyes to the leaves."

They moved as quickly as they could in their huddle. Baby-X sat firmly on Spud's good shoulder – the one not torn by the X, but Baby-X's claws still drew blood as she clung on tightly. He kept glancing at her line of sight, kept tensing when she did. When she lowered her head and those ears went back, he knew the X was close and probably mirroring her position, as though ready to pounce.

"Byron!" Spud said, noticing the kitten was looking her way. "Careful!"

Byron focused, watching the jungle in front of her.

"Keep moving, Spud!" Glossy said over their comms. "You're doing good. Under two klicks to go!"

"The others there, yet?"

"We're loading Grey now."

Spud felt a sense of relief. Grey, Tiberius and Lorenzo were safe. Now he just had to get the rest of them back. He couldn't disappoint Grey. He had a date to keep.

"Just think of dessert," he said quietly. "Just think of dessert!"

"What?" Byron asked.

"Nothing."

Baby-X hissed again and Spud fired. The X growled.

"Let's pick up pace," Spud said, and they began to move more quickly again.

"Spud?" Finn said, darting his eyes into his pack. "I'm running low on ammo. Got one spare cartridge. That's it."

"Yeah. Me, too. Try not to fire unless you see the thing."

The leaves on the shrubs rustled here, then there. The X was moving quickly, erratically. It was losing patience. It was getting desperate. That was either a good thing, or a very bad thing. Spud wasn't sure whether the remnants of Finn's klauten piss would be enough to hold it back.

More shrubs moved and they heard movement. Lots of movement. Lots of footsteps. They fired as a group of klauten came bounding out. Three dropped dead from their gunfire while the others kept running. The ground suddenly shifted so violently, they all lost their feet. The trees shook and branches fell. Another sonic boom, like a thunderclap, so loud they covered their ears, and the ground shook harder. If felt like the whole planet was shaking and if they didn't hold on they'd be thrown into space.

Then the explosion occurred.

Spud looked up to see lava bursting high into the air.

"Oh, shit..." Finn breathed.

Baby-X hissed as the Panthera lunged out at them. It grabbed Byron's backpack, as her body turned to view the exploding volcano. Byron screamed as the X pulled her backward. Finn leapt forward and grabbed her hand, as Spud fired at the creature. The X yanked hard and Byron's backpack ripped clear off her. Finn heaved her behind him and pulled his gun up firing too, as a lump of molten rock thudded to the ground in front of Spud, scaring the X back.

"Fuck!" he yelled, seeing the ground turn into flames. "RUN!"

"Spud!" Nikita called over the comms. "We can't wait much longer. If that shit gets into our engines we're fucked!"

"We're coming, we're coming!" He ushered Byron and Finn past him, firing into the trees to ward off the X. "But if you gotta leave, then leave!"

No more huddling, they openly ran for the pick-up point, ducking and dodging falling lumps of lava and rock, busted and broken trees, and the small fires that were starting up around them. They took turns to dart glances back and fire randomly into the jungle, anything to keep the beast back, reloading when they could.

"The clearing!" Byron yelled, pointing.

Spud turned and saw sunlight up ahead. "Move it! Move it! Nik, we're coming!"

"Hurry!" Nikita yelled back.

Spud pumped his arms, running with all his might, as did Byron and Finn. Just as the they hit the tree line into the clearing, the earth shook again and Spud lost his footing and fell down. Baby-X jumped from her sling to avoid a collision with the ground. Spud heard the

Panthera's growl and saw Baby-X turn and pin her ears back.

"Spud!" Finn looked back at him, slowing down.

"Go!" Spud waved him off. "Go!" He spun around and fired into the shrubs, seeing a sliver of the miraged creature. He glanced back to the others. Byron was meters from the aircraft. More rocks plummeted down and Spud saw the huge ash cloud rising up to block this system's sun.

"Spud!" Nik called through her comms. "I gotta go!"

He heard the sound of rocks hitting the windshield of the dropship.

"Go, Nik! Get airborne. I'm coming!"

Baby-X was beside him again, ears pinned and hissing. Spud got to his feet, firing. He glanced back, saw Byron aboard the ship and Finn running toward it as it rose from the ground.

The X suddenly sped past Spud, running up the side of the trees. He fired at it and watched it retreat again, then he snapped a turn and started running toward the ship.

He saw a rope being lowered down and Finn latching onto it and climbing up. The ship swerved as a large rock fragment thdded into the ground, narrowly missing it. Finn dangled from the rope, legs kicking and nearly falling, before Spud saw Glossy and Byron hauling the rope up.

Spud heard the growl behind him and turned to see the mirage charging, yellow and husky like the plain around it. He could see the smears of blood from where it was previously wounded. Spud ran as fast as he could, firing back at it, aiming for the red smears. The X dodged, however, and kept running at him.

Nikita swerved the dropship around, as Finn was pulled aboard. Spud fired again behind him as he raced for the ship, the much faster X right on his tail.

"Nik!" he yelled into his comms. "Kill that fucking thing, would you?"

"Sure thing," she said, sounding strained. "I'm just dodging lava balls here, but I got time to find that miraged son of a bitch for you!"

The ship headed straight for him, he fired over his shoulder again, then fixed his eyes on the rope trailing down from the ship. The ship's guns fired just over his head and he ducked, then fixed his eyes on the rope. As the dropship sped overhead, he swung his weapon over his shoulder and grabbed the rope.

He was yanked back with the force of the ship and the rope, slamming into the X, which tried to grab hold of him but failed. The X fell away, rolled, then steadied itself, and began charging after him. The ship began to rise as it headed for the tree line and as it did, he saw the Baby-X by the tree line watching on.

"Shit..." he muttered. "Nik! The Baby-X. Lower us again."

"Are you kidding?! We're about to be a melted ball of lava!"

"Just swing around and lower us again!"

The ship swerved around back toward the center of the clearing, and Spud lost his grip.

"Oh shit!" He fell down to the ground with a thud. Winded, he looked up and saw the X bolting directly for him. He looked the other way and saw the Baby-X running for him too. He got to his feet, ran at the Baby-X, scooped it up and threw it into his sling, then turned around and looked for the ship. He saw the X hurtling toward him, and behind it saw the dropship had circled around and was coming back for him. The ship fired at the Panthera, but the X somehow ducked and weaved using its miraged state to avoid the fire. Spud saw the rope again and had no choice but to run in the direction of the X. He just had to hope the ship overtook the X and he made it to the rope before the X made it to him.

He gritted his teeth and ran as fast as he could. The ship overtook the X and the rope came at him fast, smacking him in the face, but he grabbed it tightly as the ship raised up from the ground.

"Behind you!" Byron yelled.

Spud looked down and saw the X launch into the air aiming for his legs, but with a whoosh Spud was suddenly yanked far up out of its reach. He saw the X fall back down to the ground with the pull of gravity, then looked up to see Finn straining as he heaved the rope with his bleeding, torn arms. Beside him, Tiberius sat lining up the dropship's rear weaponry. He fired once, twice, three times, hitting his target. The X skidded into the ground in a small explosion of flesh and blood.

CHAPTER THIRTEEN

Spud hit the deck of the dropship and lay where he fell on his cut back, panting with exertion, pain, and relief. Finn, panting too, patted his shoulder and Spud clasped his hand in thanks. Finn smiled.

Spud eventually, painfully, pulled himself up to sit, leaning back against the wall of the ship. Tiberius sat across from him.

"Nice shot," Spud puffed.

Tiberius gave a tired smile, his features pale and sweaty. Spud glanced around, saw Byron, Lorenzo, Dr. McLaren, and Glossy leaning over the badly wounded Grey. He slid over and looked down at her.

"She's holding up," Glossy reassured him. Spud

nodded with relief and Glossy hugged him. Spud turned to Tiberius.

"The anti-venom?"

"Already gave it to her," Tiberius said, placing his hand over his wounded leg.

"And you?" Spud asked, concerned.

Tiberius nodded. "Me, too."

Spud shared a look of relief with his brother.

"I'd like to go back to the Hacienda now, please." McLaren broke the silence.

"What?" Spud said, looking at him.

"I'm not going back to your ship," McLaren said. "My place is here on Bracken-Loti."

"I think Grindow's Peak might have something to say about that."

"The lava may not reach that far. The Hacienda is my home. I demand you take me back."

"Spud?" Nikita questioned from the cockpit.

"If you go back down there you'll probably die," Spud told him.

"I'm already dying," McLaren told him. The scientist glanced at Finn and Lorenzo. "It's the piss, you see. The piss saved me, but it's also killing me. It's toxic, I've discovered. My liver is shot, my kidneys are failing. If I go back they'll put me on some dialysis machine and I might get a few more months, but that's not what I want. I want to die *here*."

"It's toxic?" Finn asked.

"Don't worry, one pasting won't harm you," McLaren said. "I, on the other hand, have pasted myself in klauten piss for months on end. I can't be helped."

Spud stared at him as the Baby-X, sensing it was safe, made its way out of his sling, its camouflage blinking on and off.

McLaren paused, his breath catching at the sight of the creature.

"It's okay," Spud said. "She won't hurt you."

"I know she won't..." McLaren breathed, sliding closer, looking at the creature with wonder. "I created her."

"You did?" Spud's brow furrowed.

McLaren nodded, eyes watering as he raised his fingers gently to caress the Baby-X's head. "When I saw how the Pantheras were decimating the local fauna I tried to make amends. The first and hardest hit was the Bracken-Loti lynx. Within a couple of months they'd become all but extinct. So, I played God. I tried to save the lynx by making it stronger to withstand the X. But the trouble, you see," he said as a tear rolled down his yellowed cheek, "was that the X's were killing my creations as babies. They weren't getting the chance to grow and survive. Except this one."

Spud looked down at the Baby-X. "She saved our lives."

More tears rolled down McLaren's face. "So, I finally did something right..."

The Baby-X purred at his touch, then made herself more comfortable on Spud's lap, smooching up against him. Spud raised his hand and stoked her head. "You did," he said.

"You must take me home," McLaren said, sniffing.

"Doctor—"

"There's nothing you can say that will change my mind."

"If the volcano doesn't kill you," Spud said, "the military, the mining companies, they'll move in. Once

Grindow settles."

"That's why I must stay. Someone has to protect life on this planet. When death comes for me, I will share my data with trusted sources. They will continue my work. Please, this must be done."

"Spud?" Nikita asked again.

"Are you sure?" Spud asked him gently.

McLaren nodded. "There may be more Loti lynxes down there. Life can start again."

They both glanced out the window to the flora below. McLaren watched it, eyes filled with awe. "I think you're crazy for wanting to leave this beautiful ecosystem behind."

● ● ●

They parted ways with Dr. McLaren, leaving him with their food and supplies, and a weapon to see him through the day's walk back to the Hacienda. As he left, Spud went to hand him the Baby-X, but McLaren gently pushed his hand away.

"I think she wants to stay with you," he said, then glanced at the dark gray cloud pouring out from Grindow's Peak in the distance. "Besides, as you say, it may not be safe for her here." He looked back to Spud and smiled sadly. "She may be the only Bracken-Loti lynx in existence. Protect her for me. But be warned, she'll probably grow fast, and large. Not quite as large as the X03s, but big enough."

Spud looked at the kitten in his lap. "Good to know."

As the ship pulled skyward again, Spud watched McLaren's figure disappear, all the while stroking the Baby-X at his chest.

"So, what happens now?" Lorenzo asked, nursing his still dislocated shoulder.

"We get medical attention," Tiberius said, sweaty and pale, fighting to stay conscious as the X anti-venom began to do its thing.

"And then?" Finn asked. "We killed all the Pantheras."

"We did," Tiberius nodded, wincing. "But lucky for you... the great Tiberius is speaking on your behalf... and he has a powerful senator for a father... and an admiral who has his back."

"You think that's enough?" Spud asked.

Tiberius closed his eyes. "It's going to have to be."

CHAPTER FOURTEEN

Spud sat at Grey's bedside, watching her sleep. She'd had her back stitched, had a blood transfusion to replace what she'd lost, and then she'd lain in an anti-venom coma for two days. Spud had spent most of that time beside her, waiting—once his own wounds had been dressed, that is.

Tiberius had woken up late the previous evening from his anti-venom treatment. The doctors were surprised he'd come to as early as he had. But they didn't know his brother like Spud did. Tim was tough and was no doubt anxious to check on his team and, well, get out of that bed and save the day like he did.

Spud realized now that the legend was true. His brother really was a hero.

When Spud was told he was coming to, he'd made sure to be there when his brother opened his eyes. And the first thing his brother had said?

"You shot me, you brat."

Spud grinned. "Now we're even."

Tiberius had stared at him, then let a smile slide across his lips. He held out his fist and Spud knocked it with his own.

Thinking about it, Spud smiled at the memory.

He felt movement on his lap and heard the familiar *meow*. He looked down at the Baby-X. Well, she wasn't really a baby anymore. Spud had woken yesterday morning to find her laying in a bed of shed skin and fur. It would seem that was at least one trait inherited from the X. She was indeed growing fast, like McLaren had said, and it totally grossed him out. He hoped she hadn't inherited too many more of their traits as she grew older, like wanting to eat him.

He patted her head. "You wouldn't kill your daddy now, would you?" he asked her, then chuckled. "Trust me to fall for woman who could one day kill me."

He saw Grey stir and looked at her. She blinked her eyes open.

"Morning," he said gently.

She looked at him, confused for a moment, then sighed heavily in relief. "We made it."

He smiled. "We did."

She rubbed her face awake, looking at the Loti lynx in his lap. "She's... bigger?"

"Yeah," Spud said. "She had a little growth spurt while you were out."

"Are we on the *Gabriel*?"

"Yeah," Spud nodded.

"They didn't take her away from you?"

"They wanted to," he said, "but she was going to scratch the eyes out of anyone who tried. They decided to leave her in my care for now. Besides, I convinced them she's just a Bracken-Loti lynx."

"Her claws?"

"A little venom, but not quite as noxious as the X03s, so McLaren told me as we dropped him off."

"Lucky you're immune," she said.

"Lucky you are too, now."

"Oh, yeah," she said, mind turning over. "I guess I am. Tiberius?"

"He's had the anti-venom, too. So, we're all safe to pat her." He scratched the Baby-X's head again. "This is Lulu, by the way. Lulu McLaren, the Bracken-Loti X-lynx. Lulu, this is Lieutenant Eve Grey."

Grey smiled at the cat. "So, she's part of the family now?"

"What can I say," he smiled, "we bonded over having shitty parents."

Grey chuckled and reached for the glass of water that sat perched on the bedside table. He took it and handed it to her. She drank.

"You hungry?" He wheeled over a trolley with two covered plates on it.

"What's this?" she asked.

"You promised me we'd have dinner," he grinned.

She chuckled in pain. "Couldn't wait, huh?"

He shook his head. "Nope. And actually, this is breakfast. It's morning."

"I thought you were going to buy me dinner.

Cheapskate."

"Hey, now, I'm still gonna buy you dinner. I just thought I'd better get one meal in before they send us off to fight a hundred X03s next time."

"Oh god," she groaned. "Don't even joke about that."

His face softened. "Nah, I think it's over. I think we're clear now."

"What about the navy?"

"My brother woke up last night. He's been working his magic ever since. And now he's a *wounded* hero soldier. They won't say no to him. Or my father. As soon as Tim can get a hold of him, that is. You think he'd be waiting by the phone to hear how his sons' mission went, but not my dad! God knows where he is."

She stared at him and gave a soft smile back.

He mirrored it. "We've been to hell and back twice, but we keep making it through, Grey," he said gently.

"Eve."

"Eve," he smiled.

She moved her hand and placed it on his. He held her hand firmly.

"You didn't disappoint me," she said.

"No, ma'am. That was never an option."

"Still," she winced as she shifted in the bed, "I'm not sure I'm up for dessert tonight."

Spud chuckled. "That's okay. I can wait for dessert."

He hesitated a moment, then lifted her hand and kissed it. She smiled and ran the back of her hand over his cheek.

He leaned over, moving his face to hers and...

The door burst open.

Spud looked around and Tiberius limped in, dressed in his hospital gown.

Spud sighed and lowered his head. "This better be good or I am going to kill you."

"You gotta come," Tiberius said. "Quick."

"Why?"

"Just hurry!"

● ● ●

Spud left Lulu with Grey and followed his brother to his cabin.

"What's going on?"

Tiberius gave him a grave look. "Dad's in trouble. He needs our help."

"What?"

Tiberius glanced at the security camera in the room and turned his back on it. Spud moved alongside him as Tim worked to bring something up on the screen of his data-band.

"I received this footage. It's a pre-recorded message. It was encrypted over a channel only Dad and I know."

Spud watched as his father—correction, Tim's father—appeared on screen. He was bound, gagged and beaten.

"What the hell?" Spud said, straightening.

The camera moved to show another man. Blond-haired, brown-eyed. He smiled.

"Hello, boys."

"You know who that is?" Tiberius asked.

Spud shook his head.

"It's Guantano."

"Guantano?!" Spud's eyebrows nearly leapt off his forehead. "What? That's who my ex was involved with. That's what got me into this mess."

The mobster on the screen spoke. "The great Tiberius and his deadbeat brother, Spelton... At least that's what Senator Whitlam seems to think, doesn't he? Don't take it personally, Spelton. It was always hard for him to have a constant reminder of his wife's affair staring him in the face. But you've turned out okay, haven't you? I like to think you're a chip off the old block, personally."

Spud's face fell. "What? What does he mean by that?"

"Spud," Guantano continued. "If I may call you that? It seems you took something of mine and I'd like it back." The smile fell from his face. "You took my money, now you owe me an X03. You have 48 hours to bring me one or I'll kill your stepfather." He smiled again. "You'll do it for your dear old dad, won't you? *Son*."

The footage ended. Spud's mouth fell open.

"Son...?"

Tiberius stared at him. Spud stared back.

"*Son*? He called me son. I'm his son? I'm Guantano's son? He's my father?"

Tiberius nodded. "Sounds like it."

Spud's face screwed up. "What the *hell* was Mom thinking?!"

"That doesn't matter right now, Spel. Guantano has Dad," Tiberius said. "He'll kill him if we don't do what he says."

"Fuuuuck..." Spud said, lowering his head into his hands. "Never, ever, *ever*, do a favor for your ex. *Ever!* Talk about opening Pandora's box!"

"Spud," Tiberius yanked his arm. "Guantano is going to *kill* him!"

He nodded, staring at the floor, mind turning over.

"I know he's not your dad," Tiberius said, "but he's mine. And he raised you like his own."

Spud looked up at his brother. He didn't quite agree with his statement, but still, Spud was struggling to not care. The senator was the only father he'd known.

"We have to rescue him," Tiberius said.

"Where the hell are we going to get an X03 from? We just killed them all on Bracken-Loti."

Tiberius' shoulders slumped. "We ask Quadrant Four if they have more."

"Tim, we just killed all their Pantheras. If they have more, there's no way they'll give us one."

"Then we steal it."

"Are you kidding me?!" Spud exclaimed. "Enter a highly secure black-ops facility and steal an X03!"

"What choice do we have?"

"There's got to be another way. Tell the navy, let them handle this."

"If we send the navy after Dad, Guantano will definitely kill him."

"This is not happening…" Spud shook his head and walked away.

"Your guy, Finn, he was black-ops, right? Can he help us?"

Spud looked back at Tiberius. "He once worked on Quadrant Four, but that was a while ago. This is suicide… If the navy doesn't kill us, the X03 will. And if it doesn't, Guantano will!" Spud shook his head and slumped into a chair, lowering his face into his hands. "Guantano… my fucking *father*."

"The senator doesn't look so bad now, huh?"

Spud stared up at his brother.

Tiberius gave him a firm look. An order. "*Your* father

has *my* father, and *you're* going to help me get him back."

"This isn't happening…"

Tim grabbed Spud's shirt and pulled him right up to his face. "It is, and you're going to help me!"

Spud exhaled heavily and let his head fall back.

"I was *so* looking forward to dessert."

Join Spud's next action-packed adventure:

The Deftest Deceit (Spud Compton 3)

If you enjoyed reading *The Deepest Jungle* (Spud Compton 2), let people know! Leave a simple rating or write a brief review wherever you can. It means a lot to me, the author, and really helps with making this book visible to others.

To keep up to date with new releases visit:
amandabridgeman.com.au